WINNERS

D1528593

WINNERS

A Compilation of Award-Winning Short Stories

CURATED BY ALIA LURIA

ISBN: 978-1-954102-11-8

Library of Congress Control Number: 2022951775
Printed in the United States of America
First Printing: 2022

Curated by Alia Luria
Edited by Beth Rule, Eileen Maddocks
Cover design by Veronica Coello
Interior design by Amit Dey

Something or Other Publishing LLC
Brooklyn, Wisconsin 53521
For general inquiries: Info@SOOPLLC.com
For bulk orders: Orders@SOOPLLC.com

CONTENTS

FOREWORD

Alia Luria,
Director of Anthologies

I would like to take this space to thank you, the reader, for supporting each of the contributing authors of this collection, as well as Something or Other Publishing (SOOP). This collection celebrates the award-winning stories selected during SOOP's first Annual Short Story Contest. Covering dozens of categories of both fiction and non-fiction, the SOOP Short Story Contest encourages writers of all genres to submit as many stories as they would like for consideration by our judging panel. Not every story that won was chosen to be included in this anthology, but we are extremely proud to present a cross section of the many compelling stories that won either a curator's award or a prize (or both) in 2021.

SOOP's publishing model relies on its collaboration with writers. Our model is author-driven, which means that while we stand ready to support writers in realizing their publishing dreams, we also empower authors to build their own audiences directly. For this reason, we never charge an entry fee for submitting to our contests. We do, however, require that each writer be willing to market their work and build their audience by getting votes for their stories. Each contributor to this anthology has not only done the hard work of crafting an exciting story but has also taken the power into their own hands to build their personal platforms and shape their own writing careers. For that, we are grateful that we are here to launch or further support their status as published authors.

There is a mix of ebullience and anxiety when any writer brings new work to the public. As a published author myself, I sense these feelings every time I do a public reading, publish a new piece, or even talk with someone who's thinking of reading my work. So, whether you bought this collection to support a particular author or for another reason, I encourage you to explore the stories within this collection and to revel in their diversity of thought and form. Further, if you really enjoyed this work and want to continue your support, please consider leaving an Amazon or Goodreads review and sharing this collection with others.

Thank you again for your support of our amazing winners.

NONFICTION,
BIOGRAPHIES & MEMOIRS

THE CHIPPER

Leah Smith

In order to understand the Troubles, you must first understand Ireland's structure, and its history with colonisation. The colonisation of Ireland by England began in the 1500s. Ireland would not become a republic (officially) until 1949. Before this, the Anglo-Irish Treaty of 1921 established the Irish Free State. Within the debates and talks surrounding this treaty, it was decided that six northern counties would remain a part of Britain. These counties, known as Northern Ireland, held a mainly Protestant, loyalist majority, while the Republic was largely Catholic. Rising tensions leading up to the Troubles were caused by claims of mistreatment of Catholics, prejudice and gerrymandering. In the late 1960s these tensions between the Protestant loyalists and Catholic nationalists boiled over during a civil rights protest against Catholic discrimination in Northern Ireland, and the Troubles began.

Over the next thirty years, the conflict continued in a series of riots, attacks, bombings, shootings and atrocities. The shooting mentioned in Derry is Bloody Sunday, which occurred in January 1972 when thirteen innocent people were killed by the British Army. The Belturbet bombing took place in the border county of Cavan in December 1972. The bomb was placed in a car by loyalist paramilitaries and killed two people. Similar attacks occurred throughout the duration of the Troubles.

The signing of the Good Friday Agreement of 1998 is seen as bringing the Troubles to a close. During the thirty-year conflict, more than 3,500 people were killed, many of whom were civilians. The Troubles, and the Northern Ireland conflict in general, is a nuanced and vast topic—further study is recommended if you wish to gain a more thorough understanding of the conflict.

Blonde tufts of short hair and big, round glasses swallowed his face. They called him Tony, but he was really Gerard Anthony. He sat cross legged on the floor, his parents and older sister claiming the couches. The fire was on, struggling to fill the room, small as it was. Everyone older than him was swearing and roiling with anger as the news came in—thirteen innocent people shot dead in Derry.

He did not really understand, he just knew that it was bad. He knew that Mammy and Daddy were angry. They stewed, ranted about the injustice of it. They kept the newspaper cutting, something to serve as a reminder, as if they'd ever forget.

There was a bomb in Belturbet, the town Tony grew up in. The bang woke him up in the night. He walked towards the kitchen, barefoot and drowsy. His brother was already there, standing to attention. His sister was in town when it happened, in Brennan's chipper.[1] His mam was in the pub with Josie. His Dad had to walk into town to check if they were okay. The next morning, Tony visited with his father and saw the destruction—chunks of the town lying scattered, shattered glass. One hundred pounds of explosives, two hundred thousand pounds in damage.

There's no sign of it now, only the bronze statue of the boy and girl that died. He's got a football at his feet—she has a pair of dance shoes hanging from her hand—sixteen and fifteen. She was in the chipper, waiting for some food. He was in the phone box, making a call home. Now they're just a bronze monument. The Tidy Town committee plants flowers at their feet every spring.

---

[1] A "chipper" is an Irish term for a takeaway/takeout restaurant which serves chips/fries.

There's a bridge close to where my aunt lives that was bombed. Now it's only half remnants—bits of stone that refused to fall—a divide between the here and the there. The Republic and Northern Ireland. Catholic and Protestant, if you will, but not according to Tony.

"Goes to show what can happen when we don't treat other people well." It was never about religion for him, just social injustice. People downtrodden.

·‧♦ ◆ ♦‧·

I wanted to interview my dad, once the little blonde boy, because I thought his religious views opposed mine completely. Turns out I didn't really know all that much. I suppose I should have asked before.

"So, do you believe in God?" I asked from the passenger seat.

"There's a good question. I certainly would like to believe that there's something bigger than us, because I don't think we've all the answers yet. I don't think there's a man with a beard, cloak, up in the clouds, determining everything. That's for sure."

"Why'd you make me go to mass so?"

A shrug at that.

At least I already knew that he disliked organised religion. Was it the *Troubles*? The *laundries*?[2] He and my mam lived close to the last

---

[2] Referring to the Magdalene Laundries, another dark spot in Ireland's history. These "laundries" were homes (asylums) set up and run by the Catholic church. Young women were sent there when orphaned or for being "unruly" or for pregnancy/motherhood out of wedlock (to escape the shame and stigma surrounding single motherhood).

These women were put to work doing laundry or other menial tasks for no wages—worked to the bone. They were emotionally, physically, and even sexually abused in the laundries. If they gave birth in the asylums, they had no choice in what happened to their children. The babies were often taken away without their permission. The church adopted these children out to other countries (including America) for profit. Other children grew up in the asylums.

It was discovered that in the Tuam laundry, 796 children died between 1925 and 1961. Many died of malnutrition as a result of the improper care they received.

Eiléan Ní Chuilleanáin, an Irish poet, wrote a poem 'Translations' in honour of all the women and children who died within these homes.

The last Magdelene Laundry closed in 1996.

one to close during their time in Dublin. Was it the inquisition? The multiple scandals? The abusive priests? In any case, he said it was a bad idea to give any one system such uncontrolled power over us.

At my grandparents' anniversary mass, my dad did a reading. When he was finished, he stepped off the altar and dipped his head a bit. He turned to walk away but the priest beckoned with a finger. He pointed to just before the altar, the demand clear. Try that again, Boy. Bow. He did as the priest asked, taking the lecture in the way of a scolded schoolboy. He cringed at the rest of the congregation as he returned to his seat and got a laugh. When the gossiping began at the end of the mass, he was the hot topic.

"No wonder people never come to mass anymore."

Yet he still wants to believe in something—he wants there to be a larger force at work, a greater meaning to life. He wants a little magic to exist somewhere in some way.

He seemed put out when I asked about heaven, as if his answer would be obvious.

As we entered Belturbet, he replied, "Heaven is a state of mind, my heaven is being with my family, with my friends." Nothing special, nothing extraordinary. "Should we get chips?"

"Two bags?"

"Yeah."

Leah Smith grew up in the town of Belturbet, bordering Northern Ireland. Throughout her childhood, she was reminded of the *Troubles* in Northern Ireland through remnants of bridges, memorials, and stories. *The Chipper* is based on an interview she conducted with her father on a drive home and is grounded on his experience as a child growing up during the *Troubles*. Leah is studying creative writing at the University of Galway.

THE LITTLE BLACK BOOK OF SOYUZNIK*

David Lutes

*based on true events

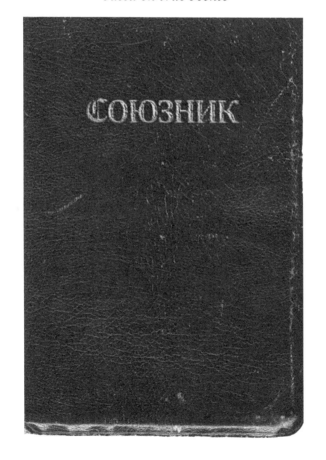

~~John~~ Kline
Special Agent

Federal Bureau of Investigation
United States Department of Justice
2222 Market Street
St. Louis, MO 63103
(314) 589-2500

Special Agent Kline of the St. Louis FBI slid the small, well-worn, black book across the table toward me at the Panera Bread Company in Wentzville, Missouri; the blank, emotionless faces of both FBI agents left me dry-throated and sweaty-necked. I didn't pick up the book. I didn't even look at it (except from the corner of my eye). I just stared back at them. They had called me earlier in the day and asked if they could have a 'private chat' with me. This happened in June 2014.

"*What's this?*" I asked.

"*You tell us.*"

"*I've never seen it before in my life.*"

That wasn't completely true. I knew I'd seen a similar book before—several times actually—just not this specific book (I believed). And as I thought this, my mind flashed up memories of all the TV shows I'd seen where some black-suited guy with uncool sunglasses got right up into someone else's face and said, "*Do you know what the penalty is for lying to the FBI?!!*"

"*What's this about anyway?*"

The slightest glance at the cover of the book gave me a momentary pause—and a small clue.

'Союзник' (Russian - 'soyuz'nik'; English - 'ally', 'partner', 'especially close comrade')—as always, in slightly raised, embossed letters with goldish tinge, now worn down . . . on this book anyway.

It was a commonly used word in the old and new 'Soviet' world of close, intimate, business colleagues or teammates that conveyed something beyond, and considerably deeper than, just friendship or partnership. It meant inner, spiritual connection and was almost covenantal in nature.

It summoned up inner belief in the other person—a bonding, uniting, joining of heart, soul, and mind (bundled in with more than a hint of secrecy). Union. It was about oneness and a commitment to another—each other—that came with a special, lifelong promise—with serious obligations, and negative consequences if broken.

The former country name, Soviet Union—Советский Союз ('Союз' = 'Union')—conveys some of the meaning. But in western diplomatic circles the phrase, especially of late, *'Russia is not our soyuznik'* was now commonplace. *'Russia is not an ally of/in union with the United States!' Между тем, Россия не входит в число союзников Соединенных Штатов!'*

So, as I carefully contemplated my next move, what I would say in reply, I recalled that I had seen the word on similar 'books' three times before: in Brussels, Belgium; Vilnius, Lithuania; and Sevastopol, Crimea, Ukraine. Each time the word was on the cover or spine of a very private, carefully guarded, confidential book—and always, so it seemed, on a book I wasn't supposed to see.

·· ♦ ♦♦♦ ♦ ··

My thoughts raced back in time. An unusual series of quite strange and remarkable professional events back in the early 1990s had led me to the point where I would first see a book like this and to actually begin to have some idea what it was for—what it symbolized. Because of the work we had been doing in the Northwest UK with massive personnel downsizing and re-skilling of people from large industrial complexes, NATO somehow got wind of our work and invited us to work with them in supporting the downsizing of the militaries of former Soviet countries. Poland, Czech Republic, Hungary, Lithuania, Ukraine—and even Russia—all were on the cull and redeploy list.

Initially, forty thousand officers and their family members from just  the first four countries must be moved out, retrained, redirected, and remotivated to reenter society and do something constructive with their training, education—and frustration—now that there were no wars to fight, surreptitious activity to engage in, or territory to protect and defend. Ukraine alone had about two hundred thousand on their downsizing list.

NATO wanted to reassure the different defence ministers and their countries' presidents that they (NATO) really cared about helping officers—especially their families—and that this transition to civilian life was for the *'betterment and improvement of a social and financial stability and peace in the region.'*

But as I quickly discovered in the first few semi-classified meetings, the truth of the matter was that what NATO was really afraid of was that highly motivated, disciplined and true-believer militarists, with their careers ending, would end up stealing some weapons and start up private 'security companies' and assist with the illicit transportation of 'goods' . . . or get into the 'protection business' . . . or worse, start mini-wars and destabilize things in and around Central and Eastern Europe. It was mid-1993.

···◆◆◆◆···

The first little black book

I remember vividly one evening in Brussels, at the home of the Senior Advisor to the Secretary General of NATO for Central and Eastern European Affairs (Christopher D.), that brought home the shady and shaky nature of 'our' ambitious, downsizing 'social experiment.' I thought I was attending an 'officer re-skilling' strategy session over dinner—and to talk about how to create a viable socio-economic funding sales pitch for the World Bank who would not fund anything with military under- or overtones. But when I arrived, I was quickly and quietly ushered into a private dining room where my host and three Russian generals, seated and in full uniform, welcomed me.

Sweaty curiosity crept onto the back of my neck. We ate finger food, sipped vodka, and later coffee while the generals unveiled their post military career transition wish list—both national and, I gathered, personal. My Russian was pretty much nonexistent in those days, but Christopher spoke perfect Russian and interpreted when needed. That said, when coupled with their voice tone, body language, and the fear-edged anxiety in their eyes, I understood enough to get the gist quite well. I'd seen anxious poker faces before. They were cutting a deal that was a tangle of awkwardness inadequately bolted onto a show of 'who would back down first-ness.'

As the minutes passed, I realized that I was very much in the wrong meeting—especially as Christopher was shaking his head 'No' less and less defiantly. The generals obviously saw this negative posture as a positive sign and were looking at each other for confirmation and for the signal to 'go on . . . keep talking . . . a little more pressure' coupled with nudge-nods of approval.

After another somewhat hesitant attempt at a defiant, final, 'No' headshake, Christopher gulped and swallowed, dry-mouthed.

A bit too long and uncomfortable silence joined us at the table. Palpable tension wasn't far behind.

Waiting. Staring blankly.

It was then that one of the generals ever so carefully, slowly, and slightly tremulously, slid a small black book across the table.

Everyone at the table looked at me but I didn't need to feign ignorance—I was clueless. That said, I was jolted with more curiosity as I caught the partially worn away word that was on the book's spine: **СОЮЗНИК**.

Not even looking down at the book, Christopher ran his finger lightly across the cover; a momentary lip lick, *"Что это такое?"* *"What is this?"*

"Ты знаешь, что это такое." *"You know what it is."* A statement of fact.

"Да." *"Yes, I do,"* his head slowly bowing and his shoulders now clearly and decisively slumping.

The general slowly pulled the book back across the table and handed it to one of the other generals who put it in his uniform inner coat pocket.

Christopher's eyes stared blankly when, all together, the generals quite decisively stood up and walked toward the door. Christopher shuffled slowly behind them—I just hovered in his shadow, not knowing what the hell was going on.

We arrived at the open front door; their car and driver were waiting. I wasn't planning to leave then as I was absolutely dying with an all-consuming curiosity to know what had just happened. But Christopher guided me quite firmly and purposefully by my elbow outside and, standing at the door, still blank-staring, just nodded his good-bye to me—a somewhat painful, wistful smile barely showing.

At the same time, one of the generals put his arm firmly around my shoulder and guided me into the back seat of the car—their driver holding open the door.

He said, *"We take you your hotel . . . yes, da."* It wasn't a question.

A cold shudder from a long-ago moment of terror found me again.

· · ✦ ◆ ✦ ✦ · · ·

Back at Panera Bread, the other agent, Agent Smith, asked me, *"What can you tell us about Phillipe Meier?"*

I blanched . . . now ***that*** was a name blast from the past! *"Not much. And why would the St. Louis FBI be asking me about someone I knew more than thirty years ago?"*

But I knew in my heart of hearts that another little black book was part of their reason for asking. This wouldn't be easy.

"Tell us . . . ." There was no hint of a question mark.

What I remembered, I carefully edited . . . and then watered it down and still further diluted it a bit more for them . . . carefully retelling and adjusting the tale . . . deftly doing the two-step bluff.

· · ✦ ◆ ✦ · · ·

Later in 1993, Christopher D. invited me, under NATO's banner, to attend with him the first ever Baltic Regional Security Conference in Vilnius, Lithuania. The threat from Russia was real, so NATO of course had to play an important fatherly and protective role with the fledgling democracies—Lithuania, Estonia, and Latvia. Again, he was helping me and my team (including two construction engineers now) not only to gather data on re-skilling officers but also to now look at the conversion of soon-to-be-unused military buildings, the idea being that officers and others could be put to work renovating sites into—and later occupying—small business parks, business incubators, training centers, etc. This meant touring redundant facilities to assess their potential for future use as *'social adaptation community projects.'*

As a result, we spent minimal time in the conference (thank God) and most of the week meeting with Lithuanian base commanders to tour now-vacant facilities.

· · ✦ ◆ ✦ · ·

A quick backstory note: Most of the *Officer Core* of the 'Lithuanian' military were actually Russian, not Lithuanian. In fact, the week we were there, the Lithuanian government ordered all Russian military personnel and their families onto buses and trains to leave Lithuanian soil on one-way tickets. Many of the families had been in the country for decades—were born there, went to school there, grew up there, married locals, and had kids there—and many family members worked in nonmilitary jobs. In Klaipeda, for example, more than sixty percent of the working population in that Baltic Sea port city were Russian. It was a tough call. They were saying good-bye to 'home.'

With three days' notice, their departure was sudden and borderline brutal in its cold callousness. When I was in Klaipeda, I watched busloads full of people with minimal household and personal items disappear down the road, headed to Kaunas, then Vilnius, on their near one-thousand-kilometer journey via Minsk, Belarus, to eventually end up near Smolensk or some other Russian oblast.

· · ✦ ◆ ✦ · ·

Phillipe Meier was from Zurich and described himself on his business card as a Security Analyst. We spent a lot of time together and more than a few times he accompanied our team to look at the empty military buildings. He seemed very and, oddly, genuinely interested in our project and in all the work I personally had been doing before and then.

While we toured around, ate meals, and drank beer together, I tried several times to press Phillipe about what a Security Analyst actually did. His smiling, joking-with-a-wink replies were, in effect, *"I could tell you, but then I would have to kill you. Ha, ha, ha."*

Midweek, we were taken to a 'no longer secret' underground, nuclear, SS20 mobile missile command bunker, its presence only revealed by the domed roof and various smoke and other pipes protruding above the surface. Below the dome was an incredible labyrinth of many hundreds of meters of tunnels. My immediate building-conversion thoughts were to make this into an underground go-kart racing center—but then, that's me.

The place had the feel of rushed abandonment—papers and debris strewn everywhere, security safes opened but overturned and empty. The Russians had indeed left in a hurry. The radio command room was a shock, a tangle of 1950s technology—wires duct-taped together, vacuum tube radio technology, antiquated receivers, etc. And this, I was told, was the command post to give the 'launch' 'don't launch' signal to those manning the mobile SS20s further East!

Phantom words surrounded by scratchy static filled my head. *"Comrade, should we launch . . . *&(*%*$*!!@*&* [static] *. . . Nyet-Da!* **&(*%*$*!!@*&* [static] *Da-Nyet! . . . *&(*%*$*!!@*&."*

What's the Russian word for *'Oops?!'*

I shuddered then—and later—especially when Phillipe told me *". . . on good authority . . ."* that those particular SS20s were targeting the Northwest UK (where I lived at the time), Blackpool and Liverpool in particular. But I supposed that was ok, since I was a Manchester United fan, so . . . oh well, so?

··◆◆◆◆◆··

But when a Lithuanian general and a few of his colleagues who were actually in the facility for only the second time, ever, that week spread out a floorplan of the facility on a table to reveal underfloor wiring and pipes, my pulse increased in a not-healthy way. I felt Christopher tense next to me.

Phillipe joined them at the table and was now asking questions, in Russian, with an air and tone of authority. He pointed at different cables printed on the plan and then to a physical cable in an uncovered trench in the floor. He walked to the trench and pointed at a purple cable, returned to the plan, pointed, and ran his finger along the plan, shrugged his shoulders and raised his eyebrows and hands in the form of a concerned question.

Christopher whispered in my ear, *"Oh crap! The floorplan has a lot of colored cables for various purposes; the purple cable is not on the plan; all the other cables on the plan and found in the trench are deactivated; the purple one isn't. It's still active but no one knows where it goes, what it is connected to, or what it does. But it's live and that's a problem."*

"Oh, crap!" is right. I shuddered again.

Back with the FBI in Pancra in Wentzville, Missouri

"That's about it regarding my encounter with Phillipe . . . nothing more to add really," I said to the two agents, with a nonchalant tone.

(My brain interrupted me again and whispered in my soul, *"Do you know what the penalty is for Lying, etc. etc.?"*)

"Oh really?" one agent said with considerably more than a hint of sarcasm.

At that, I told them a quick funny-not-so-funny backstory that I hoped would get them to drop it, back off the subject, and move on. With an inner smile I recounted more to them.

At the end of the week, Philippe and I exchanged phone numbers, and he very sincerely invited me to visit him and his family the next time I was passing through Zurich—which was quite often. As it turned out, about a month later I had a layover scheduled in Zurich, so I called the number he had given me. A woman answered. It was Irena, his wife. I told her who I was.

She enthused a strongly-accented response, *"Yes, Phillipe has told me all about you! He is not here now but I will give you his number at work."*

I called the number and after one ring I heard the very cautious, hesitant voice of Phillipe. *"Uh, hallo . . .?"*

"Hi Phillipe! How are you doin' man!? It's me, David. I'm going to be in . . ."

He cut me off.

"How da hell did you get dis number?! Dis is de Red Phone. Top security only."

"Your wife gave it to me . . ."

Long pause . . . looooong pause. Anger-tinged, guttural, growl-type noise in the background.

Chuckling. *"So, Phillipe, I gather that since she's told me the number, you're going to need to kill her too? Ha, ha, ha."*

Curtly. *"Something like that . . ."*

I never did stop and visit them after that, and Phillipe and I never spoke again.

···✦ ✦ ✦···

But back to what I didn't tell the FBI

It was about that time back in the underground bunker that Phillipe looked very slowly and carefully, pausing slightly as if reading each general's face, one by one. And then he looked straight at me for a 'meaningful moment'—why he did this, I didn't know. He removed a small black book from his inner coat pocket, took out a pen, turned his back on us and wrote something on a page—and continued writing as he slowly walked away.

Then the meeting, a tad too suddenly, broke up, and we, a little too hurriedly, were ushered toward the exit. I was bursting again with curiosity, but when Christopher paused in the tunnel just long enough to pick up a piece of cloth lying on the floor, my curiosity waned—not the least because when he turned it over there was only one, nearly-worn-off word and one symbol (that I recognized) printed on the fabric.

'CONTAMINATED!'

Christopher folded it up and put it under his arm—to take home as a souvenir apparently. The whole experience was really creeping me out.

······◆◆◆◆······

Later in the bus, I sat with Phillipe, who seemed deep in thought, and eventually I plucked up the courage to ask him. *"Phillipe, that little black book you wrote in . . . was that a* **'Союзник'**?

His head snapped towards me and he looked me squarely in the eyes. His tone was cold as ice. *"David . . ."* hesitating as if he were choosing his words very carefully. He forced out a thin, unconvincing smile and continued with not even a hint of humor in his voice, *"I could tell you but then I really **would** have to kill you."*

······◆◆◆◆······

Over dinner that evening, Christopher leaned toward me and asked quietly if Phillipe and I were getting along ok, as we had been spending a lot of time together.

I said, *"Yes, very much so. Nice guy. Funny. Smart."*

"Do you have any idea what he does?"

"He's a Security Analyst with the Ministry of Defense in Zurich."

Christopher smiled wryly. *"He's a spy."*

"But Switzerland is neutral—they don't have spies . . . right?"

Bluntly, *"David, he's a spy."*

Discussion closed.

···✦✦✦✦✦···

The conversation at Panera Bread continued

"By the way, we know all about Christopher D . . .. Now, tell us who is Anatoliy Tychonchuk?"

"Now, you're really pissing me off! This meeting is finished!" I started to stand up.

"Sit down!"

A little too firm. A bit too loud. A quick glance at tables nearby.

Calmer. *"Sit down . . . please."*

With a firm, matter-of-fact tone, *"Anatoliy is one of my best friends, former business partner, best man at my wedding and my son's godfather. But you already know that don't you?"*

The agents glanced at each other.

*"David, ok, ok . . . calm down. Now let us tell you what **we** know. We'll get back to this later, but Tychonchuk was Commander of a Poseidon Class nuclear submarine in the Soviet Navy . . . with some very interesting connections in the DoD world—**still, to this day**. But you already knew that didn't you, David?"*

Gulp.

Then Agent Kline took out the little black book again and paraphrased the following with his index finger:

- You were falsely promoted and billed as Dr. Lutes at an important conference in Prague in 1990 called *East Meets West* where known Communist leaders met with western leaders and managers to learn about methods and means of cooperation; you presented and taught there and were approached secretly by a delegation from Lithuania asking for assistance . . .

- . . . invited personally by Kazimira Prunskienė, Prime Minister of Lithuania, to assist them in rebuilding their *'new country on the management principles you taught at the Prague conference'* . . . you and Professor Nida Bakaitas (a Lithuanian at USC and a management expert) were going to go to Lithuania together to help them . . . but it fell through because at precisely that time, the Prime Minister was arrested and put in jail for prior pre-revolution collaboration with the KGB—1991.

- Spent a week, falsely as Dr Lutes, training, meeting, and consulting with senior members of Solidarity Trade Union (colleagues of Lech Wałęsa) and OPZZ Communist Trade Union—1992.

- Met privately with the Chairman of OPZZ Communist Trade Union in Warsaw; he went public with his praise about your insights and assistance—February 1992.

- *[Making a checkmark in the air with his finger]* You went to the first Baltic Regional Security Conference with NATO in Lithuania—1993.

- Worked with a Czech interpreter in 1993—a professor, considered to be the country's leading 'strategic political linguists' training center director in Olomouc—and also a known informant and former *Resistance* colonel who used to blow up Russian tanks in 1967.

- Interesting . . . *[stated with dry sarcasm and no further comment]*
- Collaborated and corresponded with Major Adam Wójcik, Head of HR for the Polish Ministry of Defense who also headed a team that trained the Libyan army in the targeting and launching of mobile nuclear missiles at Europe; he asked you to give him a job—1994.
- Worked closely with Senior Advisor to the Albanian Prime Minister (a known Communist) to plan realignment of key defense ministry personnel—1994-96.
- When in Albania, you received secret payment while under contract to the United Nations Development Fund (UNDF), facilitated by the same Senior Advisor to the Prime Minister and received a special police escort to the airport and VIP clearance through Customs—1995.
- You were advised by a sympathetic US Army Colonel working in Kosovo you had spent time with while staying in Tirana to leave the country immediately as recent US intelligence revealed a revolution was about to happen—but you were also known to have spent time with one of the revolution organizers. Let's see, at . . . pronounced Chendra Stefan . . . is that right?—1997.
- In 1997 you were contacted by the Soros Foundation's International Renaissance Foundation's Ukrainian Military Downsizing and Social Adaptation Civil Society Project . . .

I cut him off. . . . *"That's not a secret . . . that's in my CV!"*
Ignoring my outburst, he continued . . .

- . . . as a contractor to inspect the accuracy of data being reported on their downsizing of the military project . . . in Ukraine and Russia. 200,000+ officers and family members in Ukraine and twice that number in Russia.
- You met privately with one of the so-called training companies contracted with by the project who were actually senior

representatives of the Kiev Mafia . . . who attempted to bribe you regarding 'discrepancies' you were about to uncover in their handling of contract funding.

- On several occasions during this period, you were asked to take suitcases full of cash back to the UK—including by Eugene Yanchenko—who was working in close cooperation with a sub-Mafia group that had Russian affiliation.

"But I didn't do it, though!"

- Whatever . . . when you were in Crimea you were illegally 'snuck' into the Sevastopol Naval Base and met secretly with top-ranking officers of the Ukrainian Navy . . . Anatoliy Tychonchuk and Eugene Yanchenko were with you; and at that meeting, you were not only **shown** another little black book, like this one *[tapping the book on the table]*, but they actually **gave** you that particular book to take with you. And inside the book was a sizable amount of cash and other considerable 'vital' information; Tychonchuk took the book himself, with a promise to share details with you later, which he didn't do.

- During your Soros project inspection visit to Yalta, Crimea, our office in New York managed to call you on the phone (At the post office? Is that right?) to ask whether you trusted, and were trusted by, the project director, Gennadiy Aksianov, who was recorded on audio tape offering you and several other contractors bribes; the tape had been sent to the FBI in New York by the Mafia contractors accusing Aksianov of corruption; the tape was examined by our forensic specialists; you emphatically denied the accusations, insisted the tapes were doctored and fake, and gave your endorsement of the project director.

- As it turned out, the tapes **were** a fake. Shortly after this, one of the Mafia guys you met with in Kiev was arrested and $300,000 was recovered—all because of you.

My eyes and spirits lifted with surprise!

- Another one of those guys is still at large in Ukraine and the other, we know, left the country at that time with a sizable amount of cash—scared off because of you.

"Oh . . ."

- You then went to Russia to meet with other high-ranking military leaders and were showered with gifts and were actually made an Honorary Colonel of the Shelkovo Missile base near Moscow—they even gave you a medal!

- In 2002 you married Olena in the German Evangelical Lutheran Church of St. Catherine in Kiev—and yes, Tychonchuk was your best man; and yes, Yanchenko and Aksianov were also there.

- Late last year, Tychonchuk's multi-million-dollar home in Kiev was attacked and taken over by 13 heavily armed paramilitaries; he was beaten nearly to death and he and his wife were thrown out onto the street with only the clothes on their backs; all attempts to get the police, courts, or other government officials involved or to investigate the incident resulted in no help whatsoever; everything they owned was stolen; they lost everything; you sent financial help to Tychonchuk and his family.

That fear-tinged, cold, clamminess was creeping down my spine again. I'm sure I was white as a sheet.

"So, David, here we are today . . . and here is what else we know. After all this time, Tychonchuk finally sent the black book he took at the naval base and other items and documents to you here, in Wentzville, via FedEx three weeks ago. *Does this sound about right?"*

Looking up and directly at me . . .

"*There's more.* [Icy tone] *Should I go on?* David . . . Son . . . you're all over the pages of this book . . ."

Hackles rising. *"And your point being . . . ? What do you want from me now? And if it's so important, why is the FBI talking to me and not the CIA!?"*

Inside I was a cocktail of anger, rumbling tummy, and nervous shaking—and the need to get to some level of upper hand.

"Russia has just invaded Crimea. Washington believes the Donbass Region is next. We know Anatoliy Tychonchuk has been in touch with groups planning to resist Russia—and also in touch with you. Your name is everywhere in our files connected with players in the wider region going back more than twenty-five years. Washington sent your file and this book to us."

My turn to be cold. *"Again, what exactly do you want from me . . . what does the FBI want from me?"*

"Not us David. America. But we want you to give us—insist *that you give us*—your *little black book and whatever else Tychonchuk sent you . . . and . . . we want you to meet with our team in D.C. to formulate a plan and send you back to Ukraine."*

I was frozen. My life was flashing before me. My wife, kids, my career, the future . . . I was a talent management and HR consultant now for God's sake! How could I possibly be of any use to them!?

Trembling voice, deeply afraid and glancing again at the book on the table, *"Whose black book is that?"*

The agents glanced at each other momentarily and then one of them signaled to someone sitting at a table behind me.

"I believe you two know each other?"

He'd aged well—a bit fatter, greying hair. Same mischievous twinkle in his eyes.

He said with a wry smile, *"Yes, we know each other. It's been a while—and I'm very glad I didn't kill him. Oh, and Irena says 'Hi'."*

David is a former pastor in South Africa (during the Apartheid Era), the UK, and the Middle East (Dubai). He is an author, a presenter, and now both a leadership consultant and a talent management, training, and career coach with experience in over thirty countries. He has been a strategic advisor to eight former Soviet countries on military downsizing, and large-scale training and reconstruction in twelve other entities—for the World Bank, UNDP, USAID, EC, Soros Foundation, and numerous other aid agencies. He is currently a Senior Talent Management Consultant with the Federal Reserve Bank in St. Louis.

ROY MCDONALD:
A PROFILE IN COURAGE

Ken Tingley

R oy McDonald, a Republican state senator looking for a second term in New York State after seven years in the state Assembly, sat quietly in the library of the Glens Falls newspaper on Election Day 2010.

McDonald was popular, outspoken and had an overwhelming majority of the local Republican establishment behind him. There was no way he was going to lose re-election.

Here's the other thing. McDonald was an upbeat and enthusiastic self-promoter who believed the work he was doing would benefit the region. He could easily fill a reporter's notebook with colorful quotes and insights from one single question.

Sitting within the quiet confines of the newsroom's library at the Glens Falls, New York, newspaper that afternoon, McDonald was sub-dued. Maybe he was just off his game, or tired from campaigning, but he didn't seem to have a lot to say about his first term in the state Senate.

The 63-year-old, who had served in Vietnam with the Army's First Cavalry, seemed resigned, perhaps beaten down by the dysfunction in the Legislature.

If you were an idealistic patriot wanting to make a difference in your state and community—as McDonald liked to portray himself—the New York State Legislature was not the place to be.

By 2010, it was regularly acknowledged to be one of the most corrupt elected bodies in the country.

State government has an odd dynamic in New York because of New York City. Being the mayor of New York City or a member of the New York City Council has a much higher profile and more power than anyone serving in the state Senate or Assembly. That second-tier status allowed all kinds of reptilian creatures to slither through the halls of the state Capitol in Albany.

The politicians coming out of New York City were often more con artists than community leaders and the record reflected that.

By 2010, the corruption was reaching into the highest echelons of the Legislature. Attorney general and gubernatorial candidate Andrew Cuomo accused Senate Majority Leader Pedro Espada of the Bronx of siphoning $14 million from a government-funded Bronx health care clinic. It was just another day at the office in Albany. Espada was later found guilty of federal embezzlement charges and sentenced to five years in jail, while Cuomo was elected governor.

Hiram Monserrat of Queens was convicted of misdemeanor assault against his girlfriend. The Senate voted 53-8 to expel him.

A year earlier in 2009, former state senator Efrain Gonzalez Jr. of the Bronx was sentenced to seven years in prison and ordered to forfeit more than $700,000 after being convicted of mail fraud and conspiracy for routing state grants to nonprofit groups, then using the money for his personal expenses.

Former Assemblyman Brian McLaughlin of Queens was sentenced to 10 years in prison for racketeering after embezzling more than $2 million from the state Assembly, his campaign funds and the nation's largest municipal labor council when he was serving as its president.

In 2008, former Assemblyman Anthony Seminero of Queens was arrested on influence peddling and pleaded guilty to fraud for leveraging his position and accepting $1 million in consulting fees to promote the interests of private entities which had business with the state. He died in prison in 2011.

That same year, former Assemblywoman Diane Gordon was sentenced to two to six years for offering to help a developer buy city-owned land in her district if he would build her a $500,000 home for free. The judge called it an "outrageous breach of trust."

It seemed almost quaint that earlier in the year Governor Eliot Spitzer was forced to resign as governor simply for procuring the services of a hooker.

This was Roy McDonald's world on Election Day 2010.

The word "beaten" stirred some life into him as the interview progressed.

"No, not beaten," he said. "Not at all. My life has always been about challenges."

At first, McDonald struggled to find the right words for the challenge of working with New York City representatives, but he quickly found his footing.

"As I've gotten older, I have evolved. I like people, I really do, and I'll work with anyone, but I'm also very candid. What's scaring me is they are not competent. These are fourth-stringers coming out of the city. I had a higher expectation for the people. Some of these people are terrible. The senate is supposed to be this elite body. You want some people with wisdom and vision. What I saw was appalling. I saw a bunch of hustlers."

The police blotter seemed to confirm McDonald's observations. It was clear this was what was really bugging him. This was not Republicans against Democrats, or even upstate versus downstate, this was simply right versus wrong.

"We have to get away from the personal attacks, the lies," said McDonald. "It is a freak show. One guy beats his girlfriend on tape, another is rigging bids, and another is arrested for assault for the second time. This is out of control. Twenty million people are looking at us, and you need to have a certain amount of respect. It drives me crazy when they say they are a 'public advocate.' I want to ask them, 'Did you ever have a job?' because that's how my dad measured people."

McDonald railed about a bloated state government where political patronage runs rampant, and handouts in the form of "member items"—or pork—are routinely used to get incumbents elected.

"We've got to start whacking the hell out of the top," McDonald said. "We've got to get it under control."

Roy McDonald easily won reelection that night with 58 percent of the vote without any of the voters in his district even hearing those words. Andrew Cuomo was also elected New York's new governor that night, setting in motion an unexpected fate for McDonald.

Over the years, I wished that more Republicans, the base that loved Roy McDonald, had gone back and read his words from that Election Day, especially two years later.

The same-sex marriage debate had been percolating as an important issue ever since Vermont had allowed civil unions in 2001.

In 2004, New Paltz Mayor Jason West married 25 same-sex couples in front of the New Paltz City Hall to draw attention to the issue. The local district attorney charged him with 19 misdemeanors. Several other mayors said they would conduct same-sex marriages in their cities.

In 2006, the New York Court of Appeals ruled that the New York State Constitution does not recognize same-sex marriage and left the question to the State Legislature to decide. Following the ruling, the New York State Assembly, made up of predominantly liberal Democrats from downstate New York, passed same-sex marriage legislation in 2007 and 2009.

But the state Senate—with McDonald voting against same-sex marriage—voted 38-24 against the law in 2009.

The new governor in New York, Andrew Cuomo, made it clear in the spring of 2011 that he wanted to have a same-sex marriage initiative passed by the end of the session in June.

With 32 votes needed to pass the law, initial tallies showed 26 state senators supported same-sex marriage, 29 opposed and 7 were undecided.

Roy McDonald said he was uncommitted after voting against same-sex marriage in the Assembly, and again in 2009 while in the Senate.

With McDonald uncommitted, he became the subject of an intense lobbying campaign and the center of the Albany debate.

A billboard went up on I-787 in Albany urging McDonald to "support all loving couples."

Gov. Cuomo called him several times.

A Quinnipiac Poll released on June 2 said that 58 percent of respondents supported gay marriage nationally. In 2002, when the "Growing up Gay" story was published in Glens Falls, national approval was under 40 percent. There had been a dramatic shift nationwide in attitudes, but maybe not locally.

On June 11, McDonald said, "I will be doing what I think is right."

As the vote neared, Monroe County Republican James Alesi, who also voted against the legislation in 2009, became the 30th vote.

On June 14 with the vote nearing, McDonald announced he would become the 31st vote despite objections from the Roman Catholic Church, other religious groups and conservative Republicans across his voting district.

McDonald sounded like the man I had interviewed seven months earlier in the newsroom library, and his words became a "Profiles in Courage" moment in a place—the New York State Legislature—where taking the moral high ground was unheard of.

"You get to the point where you evolve in your life, where everything isn't black and white, good and bad, and you try to do the right thing," McDonald said to reporters. "You might not like that. You might be very cynical about that. Well, fuck it. I don't care what you think. I'm trying to do the right thing. I'm tired of Republican-Democrat politics. They can take the job and shove it. I come from a blue-collar background. I'm trying to do the right thing and that's where I'm going with this."

It was the type of truth you don't see from politicians anymore.

"I'm not one of these guys that lives and dies, at this age of my life, for politics," he told Jimmy Vielkind of Politico. "I've accomplished more than the average guy around here. I'm going to go and see my family when I leave here. I'm going to go, turn around, and if I get out of politics, I'll be a professional like I've been in the past. I'll make money. My grandchildren will have money to help through the problems they have. I'll go play golf, see my wife and spend time with my three kids and grandkids."

Four days after McDonald announced his decision, I told Glens Falls newspaper readers to consider Roy McDonald's rare courage.

To remember that he did it because he thought it was the right thing.

I told them this was what leadership looks like. Instead, the words would come back to haunt him.

Two more Republicans defected, and on June 24 the Marriage Equality Act passed 33-29 with four Republicans joining the Democrats. Gov. Cuomo signed it into law the same day.

New York became just the sixth state to legalize same-sex marriage and give gay couples the same rights as straight couples when it came to health insurance, hospital visiting rights and income taxes.

"New York has always been a beacon for the country on LGBT rights," Gov. Cuomo said in a statement.

The next month, Roy McDonald visited with the Glens Falls newspaper editorial board again. He said he didn't want to talk about the gay marriage vote, but then he did, because guys like Roy McDonald can't stop charging forward.

He talked about his military service, his record as Wilton supervisor and his work in the Assembly and all the good he has tried to do as a state senator.

In the month since the vote, conservatives—his people—had vowed to work against anyone who voted for gay marriage. There were constituents willing to toss out every bit of good McDonald had done because of this one vote. Some voters began saying they would never, ever vote for him again.

McDonald was feeling the wrath the newspaper had felt nine years earlier when we published "Growing up Gay." It was as if the community had not evolved at all.

Roy McDonald responded by holding firm. If people were willing to forget all his accomplishments, well fine, he could live with that.

"If they want to vote against me, that is their right," McDonald said.

"Give me 100 Roy McDonalds who are willing to stand up to their own political party, who are willing to reconsider a position he has held for most of his life," I wrote on July 26 in the newspaper. There were many who disagreed with me.

Just a week earlier, Glens Falls Post-Star reporter Maury Thompson reported the National Organization for Marriage sent a mailing to households in McDonald's district comparing the Vietnam veteran to Benedict Arnold.

It was part of a $2 million initiative to defeat McDonald and six other New York senators in the 2012 election.

As promised, conservative Republicans found a candidate to oppose McDonald in Saratoga County Clerk Kathy Marchione. She was best known for leading a group of New York county clerks in taking a stand in 2007 against Governor Eliot Spitzer's plan to allow undocumented immigrants to obtain state driver's licenses. After the backlash, Governor Spitzer withdrew his plan.

Marchione's campaign centered entirely on McDonald's vote on gay marriage and McDonald's blunt talk that voters could "take the job and shove it."

Republican committees in his district were split evenly among McDonald and Marchione and the race was getting statewide attention because of McDonald's vote on same-sex marriage.

"People feel betrayed," Marchione told the New York Times. "I've heard that a lot—that they feel betrayed by our senator, that you said one thing, you do something else."

But of course, McDonald did not back down.

"I'm in the party of Abraham Lincoln—I'm very proud of that," McDonald said in the Times article. "I'm not in a party of a bunch of right-wing nitwits. It's Abraham Lincoln. It's everybody included. And I feel that's very important."

Two days before the September primary, the two candidates met in Troy for their only debate. Marchione supporters packed the hall and she repeatedly questioned McDonald about his vote to the cheers of her supporters.

"I would ask them, 'Do you want me to tell you what you want to hear or do you want me to tell you the truth?'" McDonald told me. "They didn't want the truth."

When the votes were counted at the end of the night, Marchione led by 107 votes with 1,000 absentee ballots to be counted. When the absentee ballots were added, McDonald had lost by 99 votes.

Within days, Roy McDonald said he was dropping out of the race because it was in the best interests of the Republican Party. The concern was that if McDonald stayed in the race, the Republican vote might be split and allow the Democrats to gain the seat and take back control of the Senate.

"I believe maintaining the Republican majority in the New York State Senate will continue to positively change state government. It is important to recognize the need for checks and balances in our democracy, which can only be assured by a multi-party system," McDonald said in a statement.

There was some truth to that, but it didn't sit well with me. I knew how rare it was for a politician to stand for a cause because they believed it was right.

"On Thursday, he gave up that fight for the worst possible reason: the party," I wrote on September 30. "Just like any run-of-the-mill political hack, he caved to party pressure."

Then I concluded: "Roy McDonald was the one guy I thought wouldn't do that."

In retrospect, maybe I was a little too hard on him.

A year later, a young woman from Homestead High School in Fort Wayne, Indiana, was chosen the winner of the John F. Kennedy Profile in Courage Essay Contest for high school students.

The award recognizes a public official at the local, state or federal level whose actions demonstrate the qualities of politically courageous leadership in the spirit of John F. Kennedy's book *Profiles in Courage*.

Jamie Baer's subject was Roy McDonald.

She concluded her essay this way: "McDonald's leap of faith in June 2011 came at a steep price. Although his vote in favor of same-sex marriage cost him his reelection to the state senate, it was a worthy sacrifice. In the words of Mayor Bloomberg, McDonald walked away from the state senate with the 'satisfaction of knowing for the rest of his life he stood up and voted his conscience.' McDonald reaffirmed America's 'faith that the people will not simply elect men who will represent their views ably and faithfully, but also elect men who will exercise their conscientious judgment.' During his first and last term in the state Senate, McDonald achieved a feat most politicians do not accomplish in a lifetime—he embodied true democracy."

Between 2012 and 2014, more than 10,000 same-sex couples were married in New York.

Four years after McDonald's vote helped make same-sex marriage legal in New York, the Supreme Court made same-sex marriage the law of the land.

Roy McDonald faded away from local politics like no local politician I had ever seen before. I reached out at least once to do a column to get his views on the state of politics, but I never heard back.

When I had lunch with Roy McDonald in the summer of 2020, he told me off the record, "I don't consider myself a Republican anymore."

A couple years earlier, he had gone down to the Wilton Town Hall where he served as supervisor in those early years and built a reputation as a stalwart conservative Republican.

He told the woman at the Board of Elections he wanted to change his political affiliation.

"I don't think she even knew who I was," McDonald said.

I called him a few months later and asked if he would be willing to go on the record for this story.

"Go ahead," he said.

As usual, Roy McDonald charged forward, doing what he thought was right.

Ken Tingley was editor of The Post-Star in Glens Falls, New York, for 21 years. He wrote a nationally acclaimed local column and award-winning editorials while producing some of the finest small-newspaper journalism over two decades. Nine times the newspaper was named newspaper of the year. Tingley retired in 2020 and published a collection of columns, *The Last American Editor*. Tingley published a second book in 2022, *The Last American Newspaper*, chronicling the great work done by his newspaper over two decades and the threat local communities face without that local journalism.

LOOSENING

Chad Crossley

"You know your grandma named the tumor John, right?" my uncle asked as the traffic signal mercifully turns green. "Right before she died. I swear, dear old Dad really did ruin her life."

And though my memories of her bleed through to the present in hazy murmurs, there is no denying the searing truth in the sentiment of the thing. Years have passed, a ravine of decades separating their *then* from our *now*, and still the reverberations sing out to the present, demanding the attention of those who only hear of such truths in the whispers of stories seldom shared.

Grandpa John had left her.

There is no denying the facts. He left her, just like he left the house and his three sons, in the sandy desert heat of Ridgecrest, California.

Growing up, I never knew much about this part of my history, as though that particular branch of the family tree had withered away to dust in some dark, forgotten hole. My father never had much to say on the subject. I knew of his family, my uncles, and their wives and children, my grandma before her death, but never my father's father.

Aside from a few visits throughout my childhood, all I seemed to be capable of gathering were bits and pieces of information from others—he worked as an engineer, he now lives in Florida, he is a wealthy man, he goes on X number of cruises annually, he always sends checks on birthdays, phone conversations with him often feel forced, and such and such. And it is from these brief glimpses that my imaginings of him are born, these shattered revelations illuminating what he is, but never *who*.

In truth, whether by choice or fated design, his is a life far removed from my own. As I sit in this car with my uncle, heading to my parents' house where the family—my whole family, John included—is set to gather for the first time in over thirteen years, I cannot help but be confronted by the absurdity of the moment. Waiting for us in my childhood home is not only my grandfather, but others—my uncles along with new aunts and cousins, some of whom I've never once met. They have gathered together with the reemergence of our patriarch, returning back home from the four corners of California they so eagerly fled to. Was it to forget, I wonder? To move on from the legacy of hurt cast forth by dear John's actions so many years ago? I am certain I will never know the truth. And as I finally arrive, entering the house and greeting strangers I recognize only through an assemblage of outdated photographs stuck to the refrigerator door, the reality of it all finally sinks in. I have grown up with ghosts.

Always in the back of my mind, or perhaps the hidden recesses of my heart, I had imagined the space between us to be something surmountable, that the shared link of family could overcome distance, mistrust, pain. My very being is a direct result of this man. We are joined by blood: my grandfather, my father, and myself. But it is in the moment here, watching him, watching him watch us, that I see the truth shining bright for the first time. I feel no love for the man, no deep-seeded drive to connection. It is a disappointment, and a shameful one to admit, especially when the admittance next requires accepting.

I cannot say what I had expected, whether it was some newfound harmony or miraculous rejoining, but the hollowness leaves me wholeheartedly wanting. I had hoped for a stirring drive toward forgiveness, for some cosmic equalizer to level the field between what was and what could be. But as the night progresses and my optimism for some sort of fledgling epiphany fades, I see my father helping my grandfather with his various medications, counting out the pills one by one, bringing the walker over to the table, leading the frail and slow-moving figure to the guest room upstairs.

It is only after the old man has gone to his room for the night that the information floods in. Sitting around the table, the portrait of John Crossley emerges. I am present, though mostly silent, and watch as the image of the man, etched by all his faults and successes, is hewn as if from elemental nothingness. It is here that I learn the truth of John: the man who moved his family to the desert, living on a navy base so he could work as an engineering contractor for the Naval Air Weapons Station at China Lake; the man whose strict nature was legendary, who believed in education like his father before him, yet offered only justifiable support, requiring business-like spreadsheets for any form of monetary assistance; the man who pushed unrelentingly, who drove one son away as far as Oregon, another to Colorado; the man who could never say "I love you"; the man marked by his past, the creator of grudges, the focal point in the dissolution of a family, the catalyst for generational hurt.

It is only later, as another bottle of wine is opened and passed around the room, that the case against him reaches a fever pitch. One uncle brings up my grandmother, of how the divorce crushed her. The other agrees, saying how even in the face of the cancer she could never let go of the loss, never forgive for the hurt. Someone brings up the tumor she named John.

And despite it all, always bubbling just under the surface, there is Jim.

Part of me always suspected that Grandpa John was gay; but like everything else that came along with this mystery man, who could be sure when no one ever spoke? I remember being ten years old and receiving a birthday card in the mail. The card was classic Hallmark, something witty about having a very special day typecast in the center, and below that nothing except for the penned lines of *"Love Grandpa*

John & Jim" in blue ink. It was remarkably unremarkable, but I recall that one card vividly. The tiny, mechanical script standing alone on a page of hollow platitudes—such few words saying more than I could fully understand, whispering secrets that I did not yet have the means to decipher.

I find the whole scene to be both validating as well as obscene in some strange way as I sit around this table full of grown adults gossiping back and forth. I had wanted to know the man at whom so much animosity was directed. It was my mission to get to the root of the entire charade, to know once and for all. Yet how can this be an accurate picture? How can I judge the whole while overlooking integral parts?

Without a word, my father is up and away from the table and his brothers, making his way toward the door to the backyard. I follow him out and see him there staring up at the sky, the babbling gush of water in the fountain next to us almost blocking out the voices from just inside. I choose this moment to engage, asking my father all the questions I have yet to find answers to, praying his draw to honesty outweighs his other concerns.

We sit together, he and I veiled in the darkness of a cool December night, the understanding we share witnessed only by stars shining overhead. He speaks to me in a voice that is both reverential and sincere, informing me to the best of his ability how Grandpa left the family in 1980 on his eighteenth birthday. He tells me how it felt coming home and seeing him pack his things and leave, driving down the road with the dust upturned in his wake, like the fading memory of the moment. He shares how Grandpa lived in town still, keeping his important contracting work on the Navy base, but always away from the family. He says he left for college later that summer and never looked back wherever his father was concerned. Yes, he continues, Grandpa is gay. He tells me that he didn't know at the time, though—that he wasn't actually told until the day he married my mother. Grandma knew, however; she had known since before Grandpa left—had lived with the knowledge in secret whether out of loyalty or shame. He lets me know that Jim had died recently, that his passing is the reason Grandpa had come here after all this time to be with us.

And it is within this rush of newly acquired information that a new image of both men begins to form in my mind. My father tells me he imagines his father was lonely, how he called him almost every day after Jim's passing, how he checked up on him and offered him a place to stay and people to be around. He tells me how despite it all, he isn't angry, isn't broken by the events of the past. He says he wants a relationship now, that he wants to know his father, much in the same way I seek to know the man, for the very first time.

There is a change in the way I see my father here, a transformative metamorphosis that I know can never be undone. No longer the stoic hero, that pillar of manliness and impenetrable strength that every dad longs to be for his son, I now see my father for what he is—a man who feels, who hurts, who can excuse and grow. I appreciate him most for these very qualities.

When it comes to my Grandpa John, I wanted to be the bigger man, wanted to feel the redeeming sting of forgiveness, embrace the whooshing abandonment of the hurt—not just my own, but the living pain of my father, his brothers, his mother. The emotion of the aggrieved had lain festering far too long, brooding and steaming through fissures forever marked in the character his sons had grown to adopt as their own. The approaches are multi-faceted and conflicting in their own right. Out of John's three sons, one would embrace the anger and never again have anything to do with him; one would manipulate and come to him only for money; and the other—my father—would learn to accept and move on.

Through this secret knowledge, this glimpse into his foundational inner workings, I have learned a great deal not only about my father, but of my own capacities for change. I see the ground already being reclaimed, the progress made toward understanding and familiarity even thirty-five years after the initial break. Every day, I see the effects of this, my father trying to be a better parent, a better man, expressly because of my grandfather—his conscious mandates to be more patient, more present, more aware. It has never left my mind, the thoughts of what I would do, exactly, if placed in his shoes. I cannot say that I would follow in my own father's footsteps, that I would ever forgive, that I could even grasp the idea of accepting the clichéd tune of "bygones being bygones." It is an admirable quality I find in my father, one I did not know he possessed, a hidden secret in his heart for decades, kept safe until this moment, this instant, *here*. If there is anything I have learned, it is that forgiveness is rarely pure and seldom easy to come by. Truly peace comes only with the willingness to understand, truly the sins of the father need not be written in stone.

Chad Crossley received his MFA in Fiction Writing from Chapman University. Firmly believing in the transcendent power of words, he strives to write meaningful works that reflect the voice of the individual in their uniquely personal space in time. His work may be found within the pages of *East Jasmine Review*, *Mojave River Review*, *Ghost City Press*, *Spiral Orb*, and elsewhere. He is currently living in Portland, Oregon, and working on a new novel.

FAMILIES, RELATIONSHIPS & INSPIRATIONAL

PICTURES ON THE WALL

Chana Kohanchi

Emily sat on the blue sheets and comforter that had been crisp clean for a few months. She looked down at herself and saw the sweats she was in and scowled. Used tissues were scattered around her as she held the picture frame in one hand and a tissue over her mouth and nose. She took a look around the room seeing his face everywhere. Different pictures she had been looking at were staring at her from the floor. She had almost forgotten what his smiling face looked like. Emily glanced at the little basketball hoop above his closet and sighed. Her hand fell to the teddy bear lying on his bed, taking his place since the accident.

Emily's gaze traveled to the door as she felt a presence in the room. She saw the tan Timberland boots and the snow that was tracked in still sitting on the sole of the shoe, causing her to be still. She hadn't heard him walk in as her loud sobs echoed off the apartment walls. Only then could the noises of the night be noticed. The honking of horns at rush hour was heard through the window that Emily opened when she felt like she could not breathe.

Emily gasped when she saw his shadow on the wall and she slowly pushed her head to turn and see John standing there. She closed her eyes and braced herself for what usually came. The times he saw her crying and shouted at her that it was all her fault that their son was no longer with them. It was her fault that she wanted to work and had hired a babysitter to do a crappy job of watching their child. The times he grabbed the bottle and left the house after already being at the bar for hours—the bar she thought he was still at tonight. The way the bedroom door was permanently closed in this house and even a glance to it set him to that bottle. Her memories of the last few months came rushing back as she cringed nervously.

Her brows tightened and her shoulders sagged when she felt a gentle touch of a hand on her shoulder. She looked up, still waiting for it, but she got something different. She took in his appearance and was more confused. His beard had been shaved and his young face was back. His hair was cut and no longer grown out. He didn't have the stench of alcohol on him—in fact, he smelled good. He was still wearing his coat, but his gloves were hanging out of his pockets. Emily stared into his eyes, searching. They were clear as day. The bloodshot eyes she had become accustomed to were gone. His blue crystal eyes were back again. She looked back down at his hand then up to his face in confusion. He sat next to her on the bed and tilted her head towards him to look into her teary eyes.

"I wasn't at the bar," John whispered softly, sensing her confusion. "I was at an AA meeting. I've been going for a little while." Emily didn't know how to process that information. She could be sure her mouth was wide open in shock. He made her speechless, yet so curious. She didn't know how he would react if she asked questions. The man she had once been married to had slipped away long ago and an angry person had replaced him. She tried to remember the past few days and if she had noticed a change in him. Her mind was blocked, only filled with images of her crying and his returning late to go straight to bed. She was too preoccupied in her pity and guilt to notice that their bed hadn't reeked in days. He turned towards her and took her hands in his, placing the frame she was holding on the bed next to him after taking a long glance at it.

"I'm sorry, baby," he said. "I'm clean," he paused. "Well, I'm getting there." Emily started sobbing again for a different reason. Gasping for breath she was sobbing so hard, she had difficulty talking. She clenched her stomach as she started gagging from her sobs. Her hands covering her face in embarrassment from the emotion overtaking her. It seemed like her long-lost husband was truly back in front of her.

"I thought you were at the bar," she muttered. She quickly glanced around the room and added, "I'm sorry I'm here. I didn't know you would be home." A small smirk lifted on John's face, just noticeable for Emily to see. It had been a long time since she'd seen a hint of a smile from him. It was a smile of relief and sadness. John was relieved his wife was okay but saddened that she apologized for being in their son's room.

"You don't need to be sorry, Emily. He was ours. He still is ours. I'm sorry I tried to make you forget that." He took in the scene around him. He looked at Emily trying to control the tears running down her face. She grabbed another tissue from the box and he noticed all the used ones she had already gone through. John saw the toys that had once been in the living room, their bedroom, and the kitchen. He saw the photos that once hung on every wall but were now thrown into a pile at the side of this small bedroom. The smiling faces, the playfulness of a family that was wiped away from him. He could have kept that alive for the last three months, but instead he took away the last five years they had of their child.

John slipped to the floor in between the tissues and pictures. Slowly he picked each photo off the floor and put it in a pile. Emily stared wide-eyed and quiet while he did so. He rose off the floor with the pictures in his hand and disappeared from the room. Minutes went by that Emily just sat on the bed not moving a muscle. She tried to stop the tears from forming in her eyes again as the picture in her mind of John grabbing a bottle and running out was so apparent in her brain. She waited with her stomach tight to hear the door slam, but nothing came. John appeared back with photo albums and picture frames in his hand. He looked back and forth between Emily and the objects in his hands.

"Help me?" he asked while nodding towards the pictures. Emily finally cracked a smile and nodded her head so fast she felt dizzy. They both sat on the floor putting photos in the albums and picking their favorite ones to go in the frames. They went over memories that they had in the photo. His first step, his birthday cake, and his first baby basketball. John looked at his wife and saw the smile back where it belonged. He had forgotten what it felt like to smile himself, to laugh, and to feel happy. Before they knew it, time had passed and the darkened sky was just showing a hint of light.

They went around the apartment and placed the frames where they once were. The tables by the couch, the bookshelves in the dining room, and the counter in the kitchen were filled with pictures. The albums were placed next to the wedding album where anyone could look at the pictures if he or she wanted. John knew one thing was missing. He grabbed Emily's hand and walked her back to the room. For some reason, the light blue walls seemed brighter than they had moments before. He left Emily standing in the hall by the doorway as he went to get the last piece. The picture frame Emily was holding in her hand when he had walked in was still on the bed. John picked it up and walked towards their bedroom. He placed the frame on the wall next to the door inside their bedroom. John straightened it and took a step back to look. From the side of his eye, he saw tears form in Emily's eyes again as she cupped a hand over her mouth and the other went to her clenched stomach. He walked up to her and brought her to the picture.

John stared at the picture as he stood next to his wife and said, "Can we try for another?"

"What?" Emily almost choked as she turned her head to him. She coughed trying to regain her breath as John rubbed her back.

"It wasn't your fault. It wasn't mine," he said as he grabbed her shoulder to make sure she was listening. She couldn't look away if she tried. "Our babysitter should have been watching him in the backyard and the driver should have looked where he was going," he said a little angrily before continuing. "Why shouldn't we try again and make more than five years of memories with another child?" he asked her.

Emily started sobbing hysterically as the words came out of his mouth. He stopped talking and a look of worry surfaced on his face.

"I'm sorry," Emily said as she saw his bright happy face now turn sad. Emily grabbed the picture of their five-year old David smiling brightly at the beach. She looked down at her belly and back up at John. His eyebrows creased in confusion as she rubbed her belly and smiled.

"David, you're going to have a brother or a sister," Emily said looking down at the picture.

John's eyebrows twisted in confusion before he understood. His lips curled up as he asked, "Really?"

"I haven't been feeling well for a while now and thought it was the shock of him being gone, but I found out I'm already a few months along," she explained. "It must have been right before," she said quietly.

"You just made me so happy," John stated as he bent down and kissed her belly. Emily took the picture of David and placed it back on the wall. She took a glance around the room and out toward the hallway. She saw David's face all over and smiled thinking another face would join in the pictures soon.

Chana Kohanchi works at an advertising and public relations agency in Chicago. She has her MFA in Creative Writing from Roosevelt University. In her down time, she enjoys reading, watching comedies, cuddling with her dog, and hanging out with friends and family. This is her first publication with Something or Other Publishing. She hopes to continue having her writing printed, with dreams of one day publishing a book.

BETWEEN LIFE AND DEATH

Sameen Azmat

Ava glanced one more time at the letter her sister had sent her from another part of the country during the fall, when she couldn't come to visit them in their hometown. She kept reading the last line, "We'll meet really soon, Ava, till then take care. Love, Cynthia." She kept reading the words 'We'll meet really soon.' It had been two years since she had seen her sister. Ever since her sister had gotten married and had the most beautiful little baby girl, Ava had not had the time to visit them. In that moment, she kept thinking about her sister and how much she wished she had gotten a chance to meet her little niece at least once. How cute and healthy she looked in all the pictures Cynthia had sent her. But maybe some things are just not meant to happen.

She returned her sister's letter to the envelope and put the envelope back in the box for her most beloved things. The box didn't have many items in it—a good luck pendant her mother gave her before she came to Brisbane to study law, a gold coin her father had given her for times of dire need, a small cloth with 'Ava' knitted on it by her dead grandmother, and all the letters her sister had sent her from Melbourne, ever since she had moved to Brisbane to study.

It had been two years and a half since she was away from her family. Her parents were eager to send her away so she could pursue the career they had always wanted for her. Her parents had only two daughters, and, after her sister married the love of her life and settled in a different city, Ava was the only one left to fulfill all the expectations of her parents. She didn't come from a rich family, but she did come from a family of grace with big dreams. With big dreams come big expectations and bigger responsibilities.

When Ava was little, she had always dreamt of becoming a writer. She wanted to study literature and spend the rest of her life writing poetry and novels and become a world-famous writer. But instead she was forced into living a life which was the complete opposite of what she had imagined—trapped in a city she had never been to before in her life, away from her family, living in a hostel and studying a course she had no interest in.

"We're counting on you, Ava." Her mother had said before her departure. "Don't let us down," her father told her while he hugged her at the airport. It had now been more than two years that she had been holding herself together because of those words, living a life she never intended. It was nothing like she imagined adult life would be when she was a little girl. It was much more complicated and held a lot more burden than her little, fragile mind could have ever imagined.

But now the weight of those words her parents had said was too much to carry. Now she had decided to end everything and make the pain go away. She had thought it over repeatedly on how to end it. Thinking about her parents and her sister, she couldn't bear the thought of their seeing a dead body hanging from the ceiling or blood dripping from her wrists. The easiest way was to take the sleeping pills and quietly end everything. She had stolen them from her insomniac friend's drawer when they were studying together last month. One by one she took out 20 pills, her hands shaking and eyes filled with tears. She had tried to do this many times before but never found the right amount of courage. But tonight, everyone in the hostel was away at a college concert and she had enough time. Before everyone returned, she would be long gone.

She closed her eyes tightly and slowly moved her hand holding the pills towards her mouth. She hesitated twice. But the third time she managed to put them inside her mouth. Just as she was going to swallow them, she heard a cry which made her instantly freeze. She thought no one would be back for a long time. It was like she was standing between life and death, waiting for the person in the corridor to go away so she could resume. She heard the cry again, this time even louder. It seemed to be that of a girl. She took the pills out of her mouth, put them in a piece of cloth, quickly hid them under her pillow and rushed out the door.

The girl was catching her breath from across the corridor and it looked like she would faint any minute. Ava rushed to help her. The girl's mouth was covered with blood.

"Are you alright?" she asked the girl, holding her to keep her from falling down.

"I don't have much time left," the girl answered.

A chill ran down her spine. What did she mean by that?

Ava guided the girl to her bed, gave her some water and reassured her that everything was going to be alright.

After that she called the medical staff of the hostel, and the girl was taken to the hospital immediately.

Ava stayed with this girl she barely knew all night in the hospital while she was unconscious. The whole night Ava kept thinking about the words she had said, "I don't have much time left." She had seen her a few times before at college, but they had never spoken. You could be walking past someone who has numbered days left in this world and you wouldn't even know, Ava thought just before she fell asleep on the couch.

She woke up from the sound of something breaking. The girl was trying to take some water from the side table, but she mistakenly knocked the glass over. Ava immediately stood up to help her and gave her some water. "I'm so sorry—I didn't mean to wake you up," she said to Ava holding her hand. Before Ava could reply she added, "Thank you so much for helping me last night. It meant a lot that you stayed."

Ava was silent for a moment. She wanted to ask the girl about her condition, but she was afraid that she would be uncomfortable telling her.

"I know what you're thinking," the girl said. "It's okay. I was diagnosed with stage three cancer last month. That is why I'm here."

Ava went totally speechless. She had never imagined that the night she was going to take her own life, she would actually end up saving someone else's. She didn't know what to say. She looked into the girl's eyes. Her eyes said she was broken, but still hopeful and strong. After a long pause, Ava finally said, "I'm so sorry to hear this. I had no idea."

"It's okay. No one does actually," the girl replied. "I haven't told anyone yet."

"But why? Why haven't you told anyone? Why would you suffer alone in something like this?" asked Ava.

"Because I don't need anyone to look at me with sympathy. I don't need anyone to treat me like a half-dead girl. My father is a poor man and I'm his only hope. I can't take away his hope just now. I have to fight this. If not for myself, then for my father and my dead mother who've always had no one but me to look up to. They have had big hopes for me and by giving up without fighting, I would take away their biggest hope." She paused to catch her breath. "I would rather die fighting this deadly disease than to watch my family break apart with their hopes torn to pieces. I will not give up till my very last breath."

Before Ava could say anything, a doctor came in to check with his patient, and Ava was asked to leave the room. She went out of the hospital to get some fresh air. She wasn't able to think straight and her mind went totally blank. All she could think of was how wrong she had been about her life. Before all this, she had thought of her life as unworthy and wasted just because of a few things that didn't go her way. But the girl she had left back in the hospital was fighting a battle between life and death. She didn't even know which breath was going to be her last, yet still she was so positive about everything. She was not willing to give up without a fight even when she knew the chances of survival were remote.

But Ava? She had a whole life ahead of her to fulfill all the dreams she had had since she was little. She had a whole life ahead of her with so many chances to live it the way she wanted to. In that moment, she regretted being so ungrateful and negative about her life.

Ava suddenly remembered the pills she had hidden beneath her pillow. She quickly rushed her way back to the hostel, hoping no one had found them.

She sighed with relief when she found the pills in the same place she left them last night. She had to get rid of them right away. Just as she was on her way to flush them down the toilet, there was a knock on her door. She tightly clenched the piece of cloth in her hand. Before she could open the door herself, her friend came in uninvited and handed her a letter. "It came for you this morning," she said and then added, "I'm so sorry to hear about poor Sophia. Thank heavens you decided to stay back last night or else who knows what would've happened to her." Ava just nodded her head, not knowing what to say. It was just now that she got to know her name. "And by the way, by any chance have you seen my sleeping pills? I can't find them anywhere!" Ava just shook her head no. Her friend gave a sigh and left, closing the door behind. Before opening the letter, she flushed those very pills her friend was asking for. She felt badly and thought about replacing them with the excuse that she had some extra.

After that she opened the letter. It was from her sister.

"My dearest Ava, I hope you are doing fine and taking care of your-self just like you had promised before you left. I'm sorry for writing to you so late; I have been extremely busy with your niece these past few days. She is getting naughtier day by day and you won't believe how much she has grown up. Yesterday, she spoke her first word and guess what it was? It was Ava! Your name is the first word she ever spoke. I won't deny I was a little jealous because she obviously loves you more than she loves me and she just can't wait to meet you. So I hope you are ready because we all are coming to meet you next weekend along with Mom and Dad. Till then, lots of love. Your sister."

Ava closed the letter, hugged the piece of paper tightly and cried her heart out. For the first time in years, she was glad to be alive. She was glad not only for having the most beautiful family, but also for having a blessed life and the time to spend it rightfully.

She placed the letter in the box with the rest of her precious belongings and made her way out. She had to buy the most exquisite flowers before heading back to the hospital.

Sameen Azmat is from Pakistan, a small country in South Asia. Sameen is near the end of her medical school studies. Hopefully by the time everyone reads this, she will be called doctor. Becoming a part of the world of medicine has been her life goal for as long as she can remember, and she has worked very hard to get where she is today. But to become part of a book is one thing she never imagined. It's more than a dream come true. To Sameen, writing is what life is to the soul. She started writing at a very young age, and it was nothing more than short stories, poems, and songs. English is not her mother tongue, but it is her language of comfort whenever she sits down to write. "Between Life and Death" is a work of fiction and was written with no intention to reach where it is today. It was just a mere attempt to participate in a contest for the first time. She hopes that everyone who reads the story loves it and keeps the message she wanted to deliver safely in their minds. This story has been a great motivation for Sameen to do what she loves more often—to write! To become a part of this book is a great honor, one she will cherish for the rest of her life.

THE SECRET

Giovanni Margarone

It had been a long time since I went to see my grandpa. I was always working, often late into the night, but my work was like that, with no set schedule and no peace.

He welcomed me as usual—with a smile. He was so old, his back bent by life, yet his eyes shone with a serenity that he never lost. He was sitting in his chair, marked by years, with his skin scratched by his cat Zoe, his inseparable companion.

It was cold outside, but the sun of the Riviera[3] warmed the air a little and brightened the colors. The sea, blue and flat, was furrowed only by a solitary *gozzo*,[4] with fishermen pulling nets, hoping to land on the shore with their loot. I embraced him and tenderly kissed him on the forehead. He smiled and gave me a caress. Though I was his nephew, I knew little of him; his past life was shrouded in mystery. He did not like to talk about himself and his past, unlike other elders who, with redundancy, did nothing but dredge up their distant past.

That's why I liked Grandpa—because he was different from other old people—he was special. He had lived alone for many years now in that large house overlooking the sea. It was my dream to live there, but

---

[3] Ligurian Riviera, Italy
[4] Small fishing boat commonly used in the Genoa, Italy, area

instead I had to stay in Turin and endure the screeching of city life, far from the tranquility of that magical place where Grandpa lived. I had dedicated that day to him, rejecting every temptation to work. His house was a plethora of memories which began when he married my grandmother. Before that . . . nothing. I was curious. I was always curious when with him, but as soon as I asked him something about his past, he would change the conversation. That's what he always did. Every attempt to dig into his life met hard stone resistance.

We had lunch together—a steak and a glass of wine and the inevitable *focaccia*.[5] I brought it, fragrant and warm from the oven. My grandpa was very lucid. His hands were marked by work and his skin, darkened by a lifetime spent in the sun, had not lost color over the years. His eyes sparkled like the waves of the sea. No one could have uprooted Grandpa from there. His deep roots stretched towards the center of the earth. Only the death Grandpa awaited serenely had that power. He said it was a passage to eternal rest and that you should not be afraid. His philosophy sometimes frightened me. The mere thought of his lying in a coffin made me so terrified at times that I could not sleep—the mere fact of death, the end of being, the end of everything. No, I didn't want him to die, even though I was aware that the cycle of life was designed that way and that no one could change the cycle, nor know what was really next.

After lunch, Grandpa went to rest in the afternoon and I found myself alone with silence.

The winter sun crept in between the louvers of half-closed shutters and a light breeze waved the large palm tree in front of the house, towering in its splendor, a shady refuge for summer birds. I had so many memories as a child in that house—happy days, games and excitement. I had become familiar with everything in the house except the cellar that Grandpa always kept locked. He had said that he locked it because

---

[5] Typical Ligurian flatbread

he was afraid they would steal his wine, his Rossese[6] that he bought in demijohns every year from an old friend in Triora.[7] I had always respected his reason. Because I loved him, I could never hurt him, nor even ask him to let me in the cellar. It would have been like invading his life, breaking that crystal mystery around him. But I was a kid then.

On that day, the childhood curiosity pervaded me once again. I had grown up. I was a man, and my adult reasoning told me that entering that cellar would not break the crystal mystery, but rather the mystery would become mine. I wouldn't have wronged Grandpa by telling anyone what I might find. I would have kept the secrets for myself, for my grandpa's sake. But perhaps it was all an unfounded notion—perhaps no mystery was hidden. Perhaps it was just an echo of the curiosity from my childhood long ago, an idea which settled in me over time. By the way—I thought—what could possibly be in that cellar? Dust-covered pieces of the past, empty demijohns . . . what else? Grandpa was asleep. I could hear the sound of his heavy breathing from down the hall. His cane was resting next to the bed, his shawl resting on the chair. On the bedside table stood a statue of Padre Pio and my grandmother's photo when she was young: how beautiful she was!

By now curiosity had taken hold of me—it gripped me in its hands. I could not go back. Taking courage, as quietly as a cat I descended the staircase, at the end of which was the cellar door. I turned on the dim light bulb and found myself in front of a sliding wooden door. The lock had an acrid smell, as if grandpa hadn't been there in years. The door was locked by a padlock. The mission became impossible. Without the key I could do nothing. I looked around, contemplating where the key might be. I went back up. I thought it should be close by—it shouldn't be hidden. What reason would there be to keep it hidden? Many years had passed since Grandpa had lived alone in that house. I went into the foyer and scrutinized where the keys might be.

[6] Typical Ligurian wine
[7] Little Ligurian town

At my house I kept them in a basket, near the door—it was the most obvious place for me. I looked in the ancient cupboard that was at the entrance. Like a thief, I carefully placed my hands in the two drawers—nothing. I was afraid Grandpa would wake up. My scavenger hunt would be over. I went to the kitchen. I looked in all the drawers. I searched in vain. I wasn't good at being a thief. I'd have a short career. I tried to think. Time passed and I was afraid my window of opportunity would expire soon. Meanwhile, the clouds outside had veiled the sun and the breeze had turned into wind. I heard a shutter slam. I went to see and fastened it to the hook. Light drops of rain were beginning to fall, impersonating the leaves. The clouds had swelled to a menacing size and the sea had rippled and turned gray. The leaves of the large palm tree began to shake. In the courtyard in front of the house, small eddies of dust rose. I went back inside. Perhaps it was better to desist because the scream of the coming storm would surely awaken Grandpa. Maybe it was more logical to verbally express my curiosity and maybe Grandpa would agree. Mine were reminiscences of a child. But I wanted whatever I discovered to remain just for me. I had to leave him alone, I convinced myself. On reflection, all that remained was the bedroom. I thought of Grandpa always saying that important things had to be at hand. This reasoning led me to the bedside table. In a few steps, I found myself in front of my sleeping grandpa, and I held my breath. Zoe was sleeping next to him at the foot of the bed. In that moment, I felt like Zoe, cat and thief. It was a very old nightstand, identical to the one on the other side where Grandma had slept. It had a marble surface, under which there was a drawer and, further down, a small compartment. I slowly opened the drawer; Padre Pio's statue trembled a little. My heart opened when I saw that in that drawer there was a wallet and a large set of keys. Slowly, I pulled out the keys, holding my breath. Grandpa turned to the other side under the plaid blanket, from which only his small, round, bald head emerged. Zoe didn't wake up. They didn't have an inkling. Watchful, I left the room and rushed to the cellar. I was aware of the childishness of my actions. I felt like I did when I was a boy stealing my father's cigarettes. He had noticed but never said anything, so at sixteen I started smoking and I never stopped. My father stopped smoking because he discovered he had pulmonary emphysema and, frightened, he left his last half-full packet of Nationals[8] in a kitchen drawer *and never* touched them again.

Back in front of the door, I began to look for keys that would fit a padlock. There were three. I tried each one: it was the third. I put the key in the lock but it barely moved as it was oxidized. Then, trying a little harder, I managed to open it. Finally, for the first time in my life, I went into that cellar.

It didn't have any windows, and the bitter smell of the lock had turned into the stench of dampness. I turned on the light. A wall concealed the mountain on whose slopes the house stood. It was a stagnant musty smell, marked by time. Ancient cobwebs hung from the ceiling and caught on my clean face. The air was stagnant, imprisoned by the years. An old cupboard with stained glass and keys in all the keyholes stood in front of me. The place wasn't big. There were empty demijohns covered with a thick layer of dust, caps on the ground, empty crates, a hoe and a rusty rake—evidence of a past time when Grandpa took care of the garden. It was like those abandoned things belonged to another life. Grandpa was alive, but his world was different. It is the cycle of life that inevitably reaches quiescence.

I stood and stared . . . hesitating. What secrets were concealed here? Why couldn't I go further? What was wrong with picking up a hoe or an empty crate? I did not understand myself, as my curiosity increased and time inexorably flowed. I went back up to check on my old man— he was still asleep. I remembered that when he woke up, he'd often get coughing fits, a reminder of his past as a smoker. Zoe was asleep too—she hadn't moved at all. I went back down into the cold, damp cellar. Outside it was pouring down rain. I could hear the roar of the

---

[8] Italian cigarettes brand

water gushing around the house. On the shelf of the cupboard lay old books, including a dictionary. Then I inspected the top of the cupboard supported by turned columns. There were old dishes, pots and glasses. I reached my hands into the furthest corners, but I didn't find anything I thought I'd find. I returned to the bottom of the cupboard to resolve my curiosity.

I opened the two lower doors—they were full of old books and old notebooks. I began to examine everything I found: there were my mother's school notebooks, carefully arranged and yellowed by time. Then, at a certain point, my attention turned to a metal box, one which in the past contained cookies. In fact, on the lid was the faint image of the brand of those ancient sweets. A little rusty, that box was stuck amongst the books. Although it had been inside the cupboard, it was covered by dust that crept in over time, a sign that it had been there for years. My curiosity rekindled; I felt dazzled by its splendor. At one point, though, I heard coughing . . . my grandpa had woken up. I quickly reset the box, closed the cupboard, then the cellar door and rushed up. I heard myself calling. I went to the drawing room and I lay down on the couch pretending to be asleep. It was still raining outside and darkness was falling.

Grandpa came into the living room with his swinging walk because of the osteoarthritis in his leg that now tormented him, but he never complained about this.

"Didn't you hear me? You were sleeping a lot, too, I see" he said to me, laughing. I looked at him, smiling back, pretending to stretch.

"Did you sleep well, Grandpa?" I asked him.

"Yes, in the company of Zoe as always. I thank God I have her, she keeps me so much company. She's old like me. We're the same," he said ironically. I told him I was changing plans, that I'd head back to Turin the next day.

"Well!" he exclaimed and added, "So we are still together today. This house is empty . . . . Yes, there are only memories here and when I think about it, I get melancholy."

I looked at him. He was right about the emptiness. Most of his children and grandchildren lived far away from Noli.[9] But he didn't want anyone to assist him. He said he was still feeling well. Only a lady from the village, an old friend of his, came to the house periodically. He cleaned up and washed stuff. She was old, too. He, out of fairness, always gave her something, though she systematically refused. However, in the end, she would take the fist of lira.[10] The sea roared and the wind did not subside. The clouds covered a crescent moon. The happy Grandpa started cooking and I gave him a hand. In Turin, I lived alone in a building in the suburbs—in a small apartment on the penultimate floor from which, in good weather, I saw the Alps. I wanted to see the blue expanse of the sea, a Nerudian[11] nostalgia that I kept in me and often resurfaced, especially on winter days when that fine drizzle fell insistently for days and a thick haze made the colors die. The charm of the sea caught me even in winter—the deserted beaches, the lapping of water that broke on the rocks, my footsteps crushing the pebbles of the beach, and the gentle wind rippling the surface of the water. Even the palms cheered me on those short winter days. We had dinner while watching the evening news. Grandpa was very attentive to the news but never made any comments of comparison with the past. He always told me that this era was good for him, too, and that he had no nostalgia for the past. I felt a bit embarrassed. Entering that cellar made me feel uncomfortable, and I began to think that maybe it was better not to go there anymore. I realized I still had the set of keys in my pocket. My right pocket was visibly swollen. After dinner, Grandpa sank into his armchair after turning on the television. Normally he would start to look at something, then fall asleep. When he woke up, the television would still be running. So he'd get up, turn it off, drink a glass of milk and go to bed—a ritual he did every night.

---

[9] Little Ligurian town on the sea
[10] The currency in Italy at that time
[11] Pablo Neruda is a Chilean poet who expresses nostalgia for his homeland in his poetry

Occasionally, an old friend his age would come to visit him—a lifelong friend. They would play trumps with a glass of cognac in front of them. Then my grandpa would lose and get mad at himself and his friend would laugh. They always spoke in close dialect with all possible Ligurian intercalary and words that are no longer used. They still represented old Liguria. They felt they were the heirs of that ancient people who had dared to face the Romans under the orders of the undisputed leader "Ligurio" so many centuries before. While he was sleeping in front of the TV, I went to store the set of keys in the nightstand. I was tired too. Then I looked out the window and I breathed the salty, cold air. I heard the footsteps of my grandpa going to his room.

"Good night!" I went to wish him.

"Good night, my dear . . . sleep well," he smiled at me, followed by the cat.

The next day, I woke up early. When I opened my eyes, I saw the sunlight coming through the shutters. In the night, the wind had blown away the clouds. Grandpa was still asleep, normally waking up at eight, then warming a bowl of milk and having breakfast.

Anticipating it, I prepared everything and when he arrived in the kitchen, the table was ready, while on the fire the steaming coffee pot was simmering.

"I wish you could stay here with me. You're the only grandchild who comes to see me and you're the furthest away," he said to me in despair, looking at me with his cerulean eyes. Yes, I was his favorite. That's why, when I could, I ran away from Turin to visit him. But I didn't make it back often enough because of the pressure of work commitments. After breakfast, I took a bunch of rummy cards and proposed a game of 40 points. He grimaced, knowing how it would end. So, I worked hard to make him win, which I did often. I saw his spirits lift, as well as my own. In the evening, however, I had to go back. I could no longer stay. He insisted I stay, but I couldn't. Perhaps in the summer, when the heat in Turin became overwhelming, I would have taken some more time off, but with my work I could not foresee the unexpected and problems were always lurking. But now I had that tin box in mind. I brooded over it in the evening and decided to stay another day. Before I fell asleep, I swore to myself that whatever I found would remain hidden in me, as if I had never been in that cellar. In the morning, I went for a walk with my grandpa. We went by where the fishermen sold their fish. The sky was blue and the sea too. The air was so clear that you could see Genoa and all of the Riviera. It seemed to touch the promontory of Portofino. That sea air regenerated me. Thinking about the air in Turin, I wanted to breathe it all in, to take some away. Grandpa was walking slowly with his cane—then we went for coffee. Even in winter, when the sun was shining, Noli already felt like spring, bringing about the desire to sunbathe shirtless on the beach. We had lunch. After that, Grandpa went to take his afternoon nap and I went back to work. I took the keys stealthily and went down to the cellar. Now I knew where to put my hands. Anxious, I grabbed the box and with trembling hands I opened it. The box was heavy. To my amazement, I saw that it contained notebooks, those that children used in school in the past. They had the bitter smell of antique paper, yellowed by time. They were written I think with a fountain pen. The handwriting was that of Grandpa's—it was identical to those of his postcards; there was no doubt. I began to look under the dim light of the light bulb. In the cellar, it was always cold and damp, but I was so excited I did not care. There were four notebooks. I started to read.

"In 1902, when I was born, I was immediately orphaned. My adopted mother tells me that my mother died in childbirth and that my father had passed away a few months earlier. I do not know what happened when I was born. I only know that some evil uncles took the trouble to scatter all of the children to the four winds. I was the last of four children: three girls and a boy, just me. At that time, we didn't think much of children and orphans were just a problem. I learned these things a long time later and have no memories before age three. They tell me that as soon as I was born, those uncles entrusted me, but I don't know if this is the right term, to a couple of farmers from the hinterland of Genoa. Of my sisters, who were older, although still little as we were all born close together, two went to families in Genoa to help the housewives, while one was taken to a convent and took, as a girl, the vows of a nun. I don't know how I lived the first three years of my life. My memories start from age three when the farmer who had adopted me—so to speak—had become a widower and I was left alone with him. All I have from my childhood is memories of fear. My adopted father used to beat me. He used to yell at me. He was violent. He'd get drunk and then he'd beat me up again. As I write, I cry even now that I am a man. Around the age of four, that ogre started making me work. He had a horse and a cart. I lived barefoot. Nobody loved me. In that country, they were all crude, ignorant. He made me bring in bundles of wood and coal. In the evening, I often skipped dinner because he got drunk. Then I would go into the storeroom and steal a piece of bread. More than once he caught me and beat me near to death. I still have that man's face in my mind, deep and grim. Hands with broken nails. The unpleasant smell of his body. When I ate, I ate polenta and chestnuts. I was thin as a twig. This was my childhood: a living hell! But I was too young . . . if I had run away, where would I have gone? I had to grow up, hoping that one day I could escape from there, from that house, from that country. I didn't know where to, but as far away as I could. Meanwhile I was always living with hunger at an age when I needed to eat to grow—maybe I remained small for this very reason. I didn't know I had relatives as none had ever visited. Dante—that was his name."

When I read that manuscript, I got goosebumps, I sat on an empty crate, I went ahead with the pages.

"When I was older and about twelve years old, I began to have more self-awareness. After so many years of living like that, eating chestnuts and mushrooms—I knew them all—I realized that I had grown completely on my own. The boys in the village stayed away from me like I was the Ogre's son, but maybe I really was. I know whoever reads this story won't believe anything I've written. The truth doesn't want to be seen or heard. But that's how I've lived, and I don't want anyone to know. I'm ashamed of it. Maybe one day I will destroy this notebook. I don't want my children, nor their children, to know this story. I don't!" I was stunned, those words still veiled a deep despair for a childhood never lived, for a miserable life born in disaster. The mystery had unfolded.

"I did not know what a caress was, a good word, a smile, while the other children, even the poorest, lived better than me. I was a foundling lost in the world." I continued reading, skipping pages and focusing my attention on the highlights; Grandpa kept sleeping, I hadn't heard a cough yet.

"I endured yet a few years, while Dante grew old and his strength prevented him from railing against me; but it was too late, the childhood trauma was indelible and the forgiveness, so desired by the parish priest of the country, who taught me to read and write, I could not grant it. One night, while Dante was sleeping, I picked up my rags and ran away, disappearing into the woods, towards Genoa. Another life started for me. We were in the fascist twenty years and the city was full of black shirts. I wandered around the city for a few days sleeping and eating what I could find, until I met a guy who had a construction company, telling me he needed a busboy on his construction site. I accepted and he, feeling sorry for my condition, offered to let me stay in a shack nearby. It was a tool store that became a home to me. Thanks to that job, I started to make a nest egg that I kept well hidden under a board of the shed and I learned to be a bricklayer. When I was twenty, I went into the military, in the Alpini.[12] It was then that I wore my first real pair of shoes." Poor Grandpa, what a life! I was thinking of my own life, spent among the affections and attentions of my parents and I felt defective. I continued to read but had now passed the most tragic parts of his life.

---

[12] Military Italian Corps

"In the spring of 1938, fate took me to Noli, a construction site of the master, to build a large villa. Now he trusted me so much that he appointed me as master builder. I was good at work and he had noticed. One morning, I went to buy some milk in a shop near the church and met a girl. Our eyes met and it was love at first sight—the love of my life, my wife Tina. We got married within a few weeks. I had a nest egg of five thousand lira. Because of the wedding announcement made in the parish in Genoa, but before the wedding, two women came to the priest asking him if he knew the groom as he had their same surname. The priest, who knew me very well, explained to them who I was and those two women understood: they had found their brother who had been missing for many years. Excited, they notified the other sister at the convent who, astonished by the news, prayed for three days and, with the two sisters, came to Noli, to my wedding. I was in my wedding garb, waiting for my sweet Tina in front of the church, when two women and a nun approached me. I didn't get it. I asked them who they were. When they revealed themselves, I fainted. My whole life flashed before my eyes. The women got scared and the service was delayed. Tina came to me while I was still on the ground. After a while, I came to my senses and began to cry like a child, like the child I had never been. I discovered, in a few moments, that I was not alone in the world. One family was reunited while another family was born—mine."

I closed the notebook. It was dated 1942, written by my grandpa when he was a soldier in the war. Alone in that cellar, I began to cry. I didn't know any of that story: *this was his secret!* His stories had always started from the day he met my grandmother. Everything before that day had been an unknown for me. He was ashamed of his past, but why? This was the real mystery I couldn't grasp. Perhaps he wanted to give only a positive image of himself, to not let people know that he had lived in the most horrible misery. He was a proud man. Or did he simply want to reset his past, to forget it and to live only in the present, surrounded by the affection of his wife and their children and grandchildren? Those notebooks that I found, the objects of the curiosity I had had since I was a child, now lay there. Grandpa did not destroy them, although he wrote that he might. I didn't say anything to Grandpa. I put the notebooks back in that box, closed the cellar and put the keys in the bedside drawer.

In the evening, before leaving, Grandpa embraced me and said, "Life is beautiful."

Giovanni Margarone was born in 1965 in Alessandria, Italy, to a Sicilian father and a Ligurian mother. He lived in Savona until he was twenty-one, when he left his land for work reasons in 1986.

Assiduous reader and profound lover of literature, philosophy and music, Margarone has had a natural inclination for writing and music since the age of 12, when, in parallel with the study of the piano, he wrote novels and short stories, never published, which he jealously keeps among the relics of his youth.

Growing up, he turned keen attention to nineteenth-century Russian, French and German literature (in particular Dostoevsky, Flaubert, Proust, Goethe, Gogol, Tolstoy, Bulgakov, Prévost, and Balzac, to name a few), without forgetting the Italian twentieth century literary notables such as Pirandello, Svevo, Cassola, Calvino, Cesare Pavese and Umberto Eco, whose writings inevitably contributed to his literary and stylistic maturation.

His is a narrative characterized by calmness alternating with intensity, which leaves the reader the opportunity to imagine and become intrigued to the point of continuing the reading to the end, all in one breath.

His novels are of the coming-of-age narrative genre due to the evolution that the protagonists experience (from childhood to adulthood, often going back to origins and delving into the history of the character). The introspective and psychological component is strong, so the character always remains the central element of the narratives, which could therefore be set in any place. For this reason, the descriptions of the places in which the characters move essentially act as a support to the story without overpowering the character, but rather accentuating the story. However, this support is not bland, as the writer has a particular ability to describe settings, leading a reader to vividly imagine a broad range of colors, cold and heat, twilights, skies, the sea, sounds and noises.

Margarone's works have received numerous awards in national and international literary competitions, confirming the narrative quality, both of plot and style. He also writes editorials and is often interviewed on radio and television and in print media. In addition, he wrote two essays that reveal his sensitivity to the problems of our society.

In his interviews, Margarone has always said that writing cheers him up and brings him to a profound inner serenity. He writes to be read, because if he wrote only for himself, it would be an incomplete activity: nothing is more important than sharing ideas for the purpose of ever greater intellectual maturation.

Of course, writing to be read is a great responsibility, but for him it could not be otherwise, as he considers writing as the most effective means to convey feelings and emotions, and to induce meditation, as happens with music.

Spirituality is part of ourselves and the spirit must be nourished. Margarone always hopes that the reader will draw nourishment for his spirit from his writings and consciously experience the message conveyed through the books.

Being read also means exposing oneself to criticism and Margarone is aware of this. Inescapably, every artist who makes his works public discloses himself, which is good, as criticism makes the artist grow and mature, he always says.

Regarding Margarone's works, he has so far written and published four novels:

Note fragili (2018, second edition, Ed. Kimerik),
Le ombre delle verità svelate (2018, second edition, Ed. Kimerik),
E ascoltai solo me stesso (2019, second edition, Ed. Kimerik),
Storia di un punto e virgola (2022, Ed. Bookabook).

and two essays:

"Oltre l'orizzonte" (2013, YCP),
"2020 il mondo si è fermato, ci avrà insegnato qualcosa?"
(2021, Amazon).

More can be found at his official site: https://margaronegiovanni.com

CROCHETING IN HEAVEN

Eve Gaal

Diane drove into the parking lot and noticed the frost on the well-maintained grass. Overnight, the nursing home looked like it had been decorated for the holidays. Icicles dripped from the eaves where busy birds chirped while hiding from the bitter cold. The entire place sparkled in the morning light, as if diamond dust had miraculously been sprinkled over the entire facility.

Inside however, reality came through the intercom speakers, loud and clear. "Code Blue to room 125, Dr. Summers, call on line two, and can maintenance please clean up the puddle near the entrance?" It had poured last night, and a few residents and their guests had dragged water and mud into the lobby.

Typically, Diane Bell didn't notice the annoying drone of the P.A. system at the busy hospice. Nurses had a way of tuning it out, the same way people somehow slept in homes near train tracks. She seemed to have an innate sense of where she needed to be, which meant she rarely listened to Maggie's monotone voice alerting staff from the front desk. Today, Diane wanted to spend some quality time with one of her patients, Colleen Poole.

"Morning, Maggie, I'll be in room seven."

Maggie looked down and made a notation. "Right, Mrs. Poole—she's not doing too well. I heard the doctor say 'any day now.'"

"The doctor had to come see her last night?"

"Yeah, I think they adjusted her meds."

Maggie pushed the speaker button and was about to summon someone as Diane turned toward the hallway. "All right, thanks."

Once at room seven, Diane tapped on the side of the open door. "Knock, knock, it's just me. How are you feeling?" She stepped into the room and reached over to fluff up the patient's pillow.

Colleen Poole didn't look well. Her pasty face, messy hair, and scrawny build, coupled with the obvious pain in her eyes, seemed to warn Diane to be extra cautious. Diane had talked to Colleen, a long-time resident, almost every night for a year. The staff called her a survivor, since few patients lasted a year in hospice. In fact, the average length of stay was three months. "Well, you know, not too well. The rain makes my joints hurt."

"I heard Dr. Summers came by yesterday?"

The elderly woman smiled. "Yes, he's such a funny man. Told me 90 is the new 60."

Diane smiled back, glanced at the dry erase board, and checked her IV. "That sounds about right. Records are being set all the time. You might surprise everyone." Though the room looked like a standard hospital room, there were homey touches throughout. A stuffed upholstered chair had been pulled next to the bed, and a small potted plant sat on a table under the window. A colorful blanket graced the top of the chair.

"Well, it's no fun sitting here with nothing to do. It's like I'm just waiting to die."

"Well, that's why I'm here." Diane raised her arms and took a bow. "Figured you'd want to play cards or something; I feel like entertaining today."

"Now you're being funny. My shaky fingers can't even hold the cards."

Diane removed the blanket from the chair and placed it on the end of the bed. "Did you make this?"

"I did. I used to love to crochet when my fingers worked. Now, I can't. Too much pain."

"It's beautiful. I don't know much about crocheting. What do they call this stitch?"

Colleen's gnarled fingers reached toward the blanket. "I think it's called a twin stitch and the edging is a shell stitch. Oh, how I loved to pick the colors at the yarn shop."

"It's lovely. Did you make that other one in the closet too?"

"Yes, but let's not talk about it . . . it makes me sad."

"When you're right, you're right. The last thing I want to do is make you sad. I should be fired."

"What?" Colleen smiled but it looked painful. "It's my fingers, I can't crochet anymore."

Diane ran her fingers across the afghan. "Well I'm impressed with these blankets. They're so pretty."

"Too bad they won't have crocheting in heaven."

Diane sat down in the comfortable chair. "But they do, don't you know?"

Colleen chuckled and wiped her damp eyes with a crumpled tissue. "You're being silly."

"No, I'm not . . . seriously! Do you believe in God?"

"Of course, I used to sing in the choir."

"Really? You sang and did crochet? What are some of your other hidden talents?"

Colleen smiled again. "It hurts to laugh."

"I'm sorry, should I let you rest?" Diane could tell she enjoyed having company.

"No, I've rested enough. Please stay. Anyway, I loved sewing and decorating too. I'd make bright colored curtains and gorgeous pillows, even quilts."

Diane looked at the frail woman and tried imagining her working on crafts and singing in a choir. The thin wrinkled skin, the bruises on her hands caused by needles, her wispy, white hair, and slow mannerisms made it difficult to envision her past. "You must have a good eye. I couldn't sew curtains if you paid me. And sing? I can't even sing in the shower."

"Oh, sure you can learn to crochet. My niece said she learned from computer videos. It's not difficult at all. In fact, I think I liked crocheting because it was a challenge." The old woman held up her knobby fingers and another tear slipped out of her right eye. "Tell me young lady, why can't you sing in the shower?"

"We have dogs. They'd start howling and pretty soon the neighbors would call animal control."

Another smile—almost a chuckle, "You're as bad as Dr. Summers, trying to make me laugh."

Diane reached over and took her hand. "What if I told you there is crocheting in heaven? Of course, there's singing, sewing, and decorating too."

Colleen hung her head and didn't respond. She looked defeated—perhaps ready to pass at any moment. Diane silently prayed it wouldn't happen today. "Can I get you some juice or water?"

Colleen shook her head. "Leave me be. I think I'm ready to go."

Diane squeezed her fingers and said, "Oh you're not going anywhere just yet. Listen, did you know up in heaven they have angels, like you, teaching advanced web design to spiders? How do you think they know how to make those intricate works of art? Right out of basic crochet 101. God and His staff of archangels recruit even-tempered teachers with an understanding of advanced crocheting and crafting techniques. Beginners, with a desire to help, are considered for certain projects too, such as the delicate, random-looking moss that clings to southern trees." Diane smiled, "He's an equal opportunity employer."

"Nest-building skills require basic weaving techniques. All the busy birds flock to those classes every year. From giant stork nests that teeter on a roof, to adorable quarter-cup-sized ones for a hummingbird family, your talent is needed and won't be wasted. It's not just crocheting. Anyone with macramé, rug-making and knitting skills will be highly regarded and put to work on incredible projects. Wouldn't you love teaching some of those classes?"

Colleen shrugged.

"For example, we all know life on this planet can't continue without the pollination of honey bees. With numbers dwindling, some miracle has to happen to save bees from extinction. There are ways to help future generations by taking what we've learned here and becoming apprentices, intent on making life on Earth easier, prettier, and better. I bet God employs architects, interior designers, and furniture manufacturers for many important aspects. Right at this moment there might be cherubs creating more efficient honeycombs . . . honeycombs that can withstand pest control."

"And colors? I think you mentioned how much fun you had choosing the different colors of yarn for your blankets. Well, although God can, of course, do everything Himself, He honors those who have artistic abilities to assist him with color selection. After all, there are so many souls now . . . and so many angels. Have you ever noticed that colors are improving, becoming more vivid, all the time?"

Colleen wiped her eyes and nodded.

With a tinge of excitement in her voice, Diane continued, "Think of pale green in early spring. Trying to define the hues associated with a new shoot of grass are mind-numbing. Would you call it apple, mint, or jade? The Pantone chart my son brought home from school has thousands of colors." Diane paused and took a breath. It was hard to describe her heartfelt vision, and she didn't want to sound preachy. "In heaven, there are more colors than I could possibly imagine, but I'm sure they need someone with your expertise to select the coolest, best hues for the fresh new lineup of flowers. Wouldn't it be fun to pick the latest shade of lilac with a gradient of cream or violet? What do they call those multi-toned skeins?"

"Ombre."

"Oh yes, ombre, thanks. You just reminded me of sunsets, sunrises, and rainbows. They never seem to be the same anymore, especially with all the unique cloud formations. When you look from different angles, it can be breathtaking. Have you ever seen photos of sunsets in California? Wow, just wow."

Colleen nodded. "I lived there for ten years. California is nice, but expensive."

"So, I've heard." Diane noticed a slight uptick in her mood. "When I look at clouds, I can almost tell there's an angel with a sense of humor rearranging those clouds." Colleen's eyes blinked with interest rather than the previous despair. "By the way, did you get a chance to see all the leaves change colors this year?"

Diane didn't wait for an answer because she wasn't sure Colleen had gone outside or even moved to her window. "I hope you saw the pretty trees in the parking lot. Every year, the leaves turn brown or rust, but this year the trees must have had a new apprentice designer because they put on quite a show, going from bright orange and red before settling on a shade of pumpkin."

Colleen yawned. Diane could see she had to change directions. Most likely, Colleen hadn't seen the outside in years. "And sewing? Don't get me started." Diane's voice reached a feverish pitch. "Those leaves are basted to the trees, hoping to withstand November winds."

"Basted?"

"Yes, the intricate wisteria, the rosemary with those tiny lavender blossoms, the complex petals . . . once the colors are selected, the stitching begins. There's so much work to do, it's inconceivable." Diane exhaled, blowing her bangs off her forehead, as if the thought of all the work made her exhausted.

"God has angelic painters decorating seashells, rocks, and pine cones, not to mention animal and reptile markings. Zebras, giraffes, and Dalmatians—it might look random—but it's not. There's a giant staff of artisans working full time on feathers. And butterflies, don't forget the butterflies. I would love to learn how to paint a butterfly wing." Diane sighed, as her mind wandered into a memory of her spring garden.

"There's a fashionable, tiny bird hanging out in my yard with a teal, metallic-painted throat. The rest of him is brown and tan. It's mesmerizing, mostly because I've never seen that color before. Not in a box of 200 crayons, not in a museum, and never in my lifetime. All I can figure is it's a new shade for this year, invented by God and now part of His ginormous palette."

Diane's heart raced with enthusiasm as she told Colleen about her inner beliefs and yet, a slight shadow of doubt crept into her head. Maybe Colleen didn't share the same faith. When Diane thought of God's Kingdom, she visualized the 'many mansions,' which gave her confidence. Someday, she'd have a place to go, and so would this poor old woman.

"I can only hope that He'll find me a place someday. I mean, I can't sing, paint, sew, or crochet. Sheesh, maybe it's time I took up a hobby so I can develop my talents."

"Your talent is with people," Colleen whispered.

Diane bent closer. "Excuse me?"

"Your talent is with people. Maybe you'll be an official greeter, up there with St. Peter." She pointed at the ceiling.

"I like that . . . so nice of you to say . . . thanks." Colleen looked exhausted. "Would you like to take a nap?"

"First, I need to thank you for reminding me about crocheting in Heaven. I'm ready to teach those classes." Colleen closed her eyes and seconds later, she began to snore.

"Well, I'm convinced it's true," Diane said in a soft voice. Slowly, she unclasped her hand, stood up, and pulled the crocheted blanket over the sleeping woman. On her way out, she whispered, "see you tomorrow."

Sadly, Maggie called her that night to tell her Mrs. Poole, in room seven, had passed away. According to Maggie, the woman had left a note scrawled onto a small piece of paper. It said, "Diane, I'd like for you to have the turquoise and russet crocheted blanket in the closet. Thank you again, and hope to see you someday."

After a long career in advertising, Eve Gaal writes stories, poems, and novels. Her work has appeared in anthologies, magazines, and online. Her hobbies include swimming, cooking, crocheting, and reading. Unfortunately, she spends too much time chasing her super speedy little rescue, an Italian Greyhound-mix with green eyes, set on sneaky levels of trouble. www.evegaal.com

BLACK AND BENEVOLENT IS THE DARK

Ngoma M. A. S. Bishop

The constant drifting in and out of consciousness, punctuated by alternating nightmares and ecstatic dreams, had long since made it impossible for Kwame to get a firm grip on reality. It was therefore inevitable that he would eventually make the subconscious decision to stop trying. In this his final chapter, no one ever came to visit him. It would not have mattered if they had because he no longer had the ability or will to recall even the smallest memory of family, friends or acquaintances—not even of his parents, whoever or wherever they may be. If he had ever had knowledge of the fact that his father had died of a broken heart exactly one year after his mother perished giving birth to him, he no longer did. In his more lucid moments though, he could still discern the difference between his laboured breathing along with the erratic beating of his heart, and the steady pulsating rhythms of the machines that continually monitored and regulated several of his vital organs. Occasionally he would be aware of uniformed figures moving like vague shadows between his and the other beds. However, whether semi-conscious or heavily sedated, dreaming or tormented by day or nighttime demons, he would of late often see an unusually large lesser black-backed gull perched on a branch of a tall horse chestnut tree outside the hospital window. When not foraging for food or stealing it from pigeons and other small birds, the other gulls, mainly black-headed ones, would throughout night and day fly around in a state of extreme agitation, screeching or squawking in play, engaged in mating rituals, tutoring their fledgling chicks, or viciously defending their brood from other hungry and cannibalistic gulls. They seemed totally oblivious to the solitary bird that steadfastly sat there silently and sentinel-like, ever watchful. Yet it wasn't that the other birds ignored the lesser black-backed gull. The fact is they just didn't see her at all. Head cocked to one side with an attentiveness that seemed almost maternal, the bird continually switched its gaze from the third-floor window of the hospital, to one on the fourth floor and back again. Watching and waiting.

The debilitating and irreversible brain disease meant that Kwame's mind was now permanently confused. Yet on some level, he was acutely aware that the darkness was fast approaching and sometimes flashes of recollections in no chronological order would penetrate his confusion. In one of those occasional and random memories, he recalled that it had once been put to him that the dark is not evil. He vaguely remembered that he had to think about that for a while, because whilst he had never consciously thought that it was, whether through indoctrination or instinct, he had for almost all of his life been morbidly afraid of the dark, even when it had not had him all to itself. Pretty soon he had grown to be as afraid of it as he was of death. In fact, in the small degree of conscious awareness his mind still retained, death, darkness and evil were now so inextricably linked that each of the three seemed merely to be one of the other two in a different costume. All this fear had been a major contributor to his remaining childless, for he had never had any desire to pass on such a macabre birthright. Even though he had never understood what any of his ancestors could possibly have done to deserve such a terrible curse, he was from a young age clear that the continual mental and psychological trauma handed down through his bloodline would stop with him.

Despite his fear of it, even with the passing of time, Kwame had, on a deeper level, never forgotten that the darkness had been his sustenance throughout his antenatal experience and his morphing into his birthed form. During his preparation for the light that had made him blink from the onset and caused him to wear spectacles from the age of four, the friendly darkness of the womb had been his refuge. He remembered also that it had always been a comforting presence when the light was too intense or showed him realities he would sooner not have been shown. It seemed that from the point of his transitioning, the dark had during both night and day enabled him to process what the not-dark had uncovered, ensuring that he did not lose his mind—at least not totally, and not earlier than his family history suggested he would. Yet, as he used to reflect, dark was generally represented as the polar opposite of good in so much of what he had heard, read or seen. In all of the faiths, mythologies and stories he had been exposed to during his formative years, darkness had been so negatively portrayed that no matter how much good it had done him and regardless of the fact that it had never harmed him in any way whatsoever, he had come to regard it with deep dread. Dark is not evil he used to tell himself again and again. It was just the alternative state that provided a much needed balance to light. Sure, it is often used as cover by perpetrators of evil, but then again so is light, and just as light is a necessary and intrinsic good, so too is the dark. He had accepted it as truth that darkness could sometimes enable fear. Well, so what? Fear is not always a terrible thing, essential as it is for self-preservation. He had understood that light—natural or otherwise—is oftentimes also the haven of the evil doer. Since he had known these things, why then had he so often felt the need to continually contemplate the matter? It was as if he had to convince himself that darkness, and therefore he with his ebony skin, was not intrinsically evil.

Now, lying there all alone in the semi-darkness, neither awake nor asleep but on the periphery of both, he was, for the first time that he could recall, totally free from even a trace of fear. Even though he sensed that death and maybe eternal darkness were beckoning, he strove to reconcile the nowness of himself and the various aspects of his past with whatever if anything the future might have in store for him. As his time drew nearer, it became harder and harder for him to focus. The darkest light and the brightest dark he had ever known both began to envelop him, bringing with them beautiful voices whose melodious word-song merged with the accompaniment of ancient African drum-song. Although he was weary almost beyond endurance, he sensed that a smile had worked its way upward from his lips to his eyes and deeply into his very soul. He happily embraced the dark, the light and the music, for at long last he truly understood how it was. This ethereal knowledge experience filled him with a joy previously unknown to him in his relatively brief stay in this realm. He closed his eyes to rest for a while and enjoy the experience more fully. The instant that he did so, that particular slice of the eternal energy source that for sixty-three years had been made manifest as him, dissipated. As he absorbed and was absorbed by the cosmic energy, his healing was completed. Time and the universe, as he had thought he understood them, now ceased to make any sense at all, whilst paradoxically becoming crystal clear. Deliverance was at hand. The machine monitoring his heartbeat flat-lined and he was finally liberated. So it was that a different and as yet inexplicable paradigm had become a new but ancient reality.

At that precise moment in the maternity ward on the floor directly above, a fresh life was released into this world as a sentient being. The harsh glare of sunlight filtering through the window made the new-comer blink. It would be awhile before she could make any sense of this strange and different world she had entered. All conscious knowledge of any previous existences had evaporated. All that remained were genetically coded memories.

It cannot be known for certain to what extent she was aware of the two lesser black-backed gulls that had appeared just outside the window nearest to her. One of them had floated up with supreme confidence, the other with rather less confidence as if flying was for it a new experience. Both remained almost motionless in the air, positioned seemingly to minimise the glare in the sensitive eyes of the newly arrived infant. The momentary frown on the baby's face was replaced by a smile as if in recognition and appreciation of this kind act. The irritated crying with which she had announced her presence in the world stopped abruptly as the dark shadows cast by the two out-stretched pairs of wings dimmed the light entering the room, providing her with comfort. With a contented expression the newbie fell asleep on her mother's chest, secure in the dark cleft between her breasts from where she knew instinctively that she would obtain sustenance. She would rest there awhile and, upon waking and feeding, would see what she would see and remember what she could. Her emotionally and physically drained mother likewise drifted off to a calm, blissful sleep. The husband and father sat and watched them both for a half hour or so with the most serene expression on his face. Then, also exhausted, he gently kissed the lips of his mahogany-coloured wife and the forehead of his ebony-shaded daughter, before sinking into the chair where he had spent most of the last fourteen hours, to rest for a while in the quiet, dark, peaceful and benevolent blackness.

Ngoma Bishop was born in Barbados but has resided in London since 1963. His wide range of skills and interests includes community activism and organizing. He is also a Pan Afrikanist and campaigner for Afrikan and Caribbean reparations. Creative wise, he is a published novelist, short story writer, songwriter and poet (often performing), a creative writers' workshop facilitator (targeted to a wide range of ages and cultural backgrounds, including those with mild dementia), an event organizer and experienced compere. Ngoma still finds time to be a keen gardener and doting grandfather.

HISTORICAL
FICTION & ADVENTURE

TALES OF HUNGER IN THE FOREST OF DEATH

Amrita Chatterjee

The night sky above the forest donned a sheet of black silk. The stars glittered in the sprawling canopy while the moon cast its shadow on the gleaming river below that ruled the land surrounding it. It ravished and ravaged the chain of islands that lay scattered around its sprawling presence. They were nothing more than a cluster of weaklings that lay prostrate, staring helplessly at the changing moods of the river.

It is from one of these islands that Sheeba heard the bleat of a goat. She raised her massive head and perked up her ears. A deep groan emanated from her as she stood up on her front legs, listening intently. The sound waded the waters and reached her once again. She got up on all fours now. Her orange, velvety skin bristled and throbbed in anticipation of a kill. Stealthily she moved towards the river, placing her feet carefully on the wet muddy floor of the forest, making sure to avoid the hard spindly bristles of the breathing roots poking out from below like spikes.

The mud was deep and soft, so much so that in places Sheeba sank to her mid thighs. Slowly and carefully she reached the bank only to find her path blocked. A flimsy net stretched across the tall bamboo frames, creating an obstruction that Sheeba would not tolerate.

She growled in anger.

The hunger in her belly grew more intense. Moreover, her cubs were getting restless having gone without food since morning, and Sheeba knew she had to break through this hindrance. She struck out with her left paw. The frame quivered but stood its ground. Sheeba retracted a few steps and lunged at the frame with her full might. The whole frame, held together with only bamboo poles, came crashing down with her weight.

Standing on the mangled remains of her adversary, Sheeba sniffed the air around her. The heady sticky fragrance of *Khalsi* flowers filled the air. Sheeba moved forward stealthily and stood atop the prop roots of the trees and surveyed the land.

Born in these jungles, she had learnt from an early age that fear would not allow her to survive. She would often watch the humans enter the jungles and follow their trail from behind the *Kenkra* leaves. There were times when she ignored them, but there were also moments when hunger drove her mad and she had to hunt these beasts who were neither frisky as the chital nor dangerous as the sharp-toothed boars.

Sheeba moved closer to the river and stepped gingerly into its cool waters. She knew she was risking her life because the river was full of the deadly water monsters who might devour her. She had lost one of her cubs to these hungry reptiles. Though she had put up a brave fight, she had to give up in the end. The scar on the left side of her face was a reminder of the ways in which it had lashed out with its tail at Sheeba to prevent her from snatching its prey from its jaws.

This jungle, Sheeba knew, had no laws. Neither for man nor for beast. In this land of uncertainties, both are equally vulnerable. Might is the only way one could survive these harsh terrains.

Without thinking, Sheeba dived into the water and swam towards the village. The lights grew larger as she inched towards land pushing forward with more force. If she returned alive with food, her cubs would eat, or else they would perish. That made her push forward harder with stronger strokes. The current was incredibly strong, but Sheeba knew how to traverse it and avoid being caught in it. She had navigated this treacherous river many times and each time was laborious and straining. Every time she treaded these waters, she wondered whether she would come out alive.

There were times during the day when she would avoid coming close to the river. The sound of boats and human voices would warn her to stay away. She would look at them from within the long leaves of the *Hental* bushes, her amber eyes following them as the boats moved out of her vicinity. She knew they were thirsting for one glimpse of her. However, she chose to disappoint them. She detested their gaping looks. It disturbed her peace and unsettled her mind. It made her angry to think she was merely an object of entertainment to them. Sheeba was the Queen of these lands. She had always roamed these rugged routes on her own free will and nobody could dictate her trails.

There were days when, driven with hunger, she would be forced to come out of her hiding and then the excitement would heighten. In all the cacophony that followed, Sheeba would sometimes be forced to let her prey escape.

However, today, though she was treading into the land of the humans, she would not let anything come in her way of getting food for her family. Sheeba focused intently on the approaching land and prepared for the battle ahead.

·•◆◆◆•·

Arati was at the little pond cut out into her backyard cleaning the dishes for the night. Her son was already in bed fast asleep. The little boy was just six months when Bittu, Arati's husband, had ventured into the forest to collect honey, never to return. People who were with him narrated horrific details of how the tiger first mauled him and then dragged him away. Neighbours shunned her as she was deemed to have incurred the wrath of *Bonbibi*, the forest goddess who had hence refused to protect her family from *Dakshin Rai,* the local name for the tiger. Ostracized by her own community as a *Bagh Bidhoba* or the tiger widow, she had moved her family to an isolated part of the island.

It had been barely six months since her husband died, when the burning pangs of hunger forced Arati to turn a mute ear to every abuse and ridicule and step out to earn her bread. Her father was a fisherman and had taught her how to row a boat, throw a net into the rivers and pull it in when it was heavy with catch.

She decided to try her hand at that. She still remembered the first day when she set off into the river, leaving her son in the care of her mother-in-law. The thin gaunt frame of the elder woman stared blankly at the departing boat. Life in these difficult terrains had hardened her as well. Like every other inhabitant of these desperate lands, she too believed that hunger was the critical need that had to be satiated and, for that, even the risk of death could be ignored.

It was difficult to get a good catch and Arati had to move deeper into the forested areas. The forests were thicker here, and the water was more dangerous. She was fully exposed to the perils of tiger and crocodile attacks. She shivered as she remembered the time when she had seen a young boy of 12 being dragged off by a crocodile into the river in a boat before her. She stood transfixed as she watched the men in the boat try their best, but they were no match for the huge beast. Its teeth with the power of a hundred grinding stones mashed the boy's bones into powder within seconds, and all they were left with was a red ripple in the water.

Arati sighed as she got up with her utensils and stood looking out into the river beyond her small cottage. This was the third one she had built after the last cyclone. It was right on the edge of the river, far removed from all the other huts in her village. She knew it was risky as it was prone to tiger attacks, but this was the only place she could afford. The river lay sprawled out in front of her, beyond where her eyes could see. The patchwork of islands that bordered its breadth glittered in the distance.

At one corner of the river, the village would end and the forest would start. The Sunderbans, known for the prominence of the *Sundri* trees, was where Arati had grown up. The large mangrove forest lay at the delta of the three rivers—*Meghna, Brahmaputra* and *Ganges*—where they met the Bay of Bengal. Arati could rattle away the names of the huge variety of trees that populated these forests and the multiple smaller rivers that criss-crossed these lands.

Over the years, the *Sundri* trees grew lesser in number as the water became increasingly salty. The sea was moving into their waters at a threateningly fast pace. Fish were also getting scarce.

For Arati and the inhabitants of the neighbouring islands, the river and the forest were their lifeline. It was their source of livelihood but also the biggest threat to their lives. They revered them as well as feared them. As storms lashed across their villages with regular frequencies, the river would rise above their heads, submerging villages and swallowing them up in its depths. When the water receded, they would be left with the bloated bodies of friends and family members floating around. The water would drag the bodies away before they could pull them to land.

Lost in her thoughts, Arati was alerted by a slight sound from the direction of her hut. It made her turn around sharply.

It was dark.

A small lamp burning in her son's room was the only source of light. Arati moved slowly towards her house, cautious of any danger lurking in the darkness. Her hut was a small enclosure made up of two rooms—one in which her mother-in-law slept and the other where she slept with her son. They cooked in the open and the little mud stove was already doused.

Behind her hut there was a small fenced out area where Arati kept a few goats and a pen for chickens. As she moved towards this, she heard the goats bleating restlessly. An unusual clucking from the hens alerted her to danger. She stopped to pick up the scythe before moving ahead. Just as she turned the corner, Arati stopped dead as she found herself looking into the amber eyes of a full-grown tigress!

· · ◆ ◆ ◆ ◆ ◆ · ·

Sheeba had just raised herself from the waters and was moving stealthily towards the goats when she saw the woman staring at her. She stood still waiting to see how the human would react. Her years of living with the two-legged beasts had taught her something about them. She knew they, like her, had been rid of fear a long time ago. But there were still some who could be scared away. However, this woman did not seem to be among them.

For a moment Arati stood transfixed, the tigress stood looking at her. Water dripped from her mighty flanks. Slowly and very cautiously, she saw it move its front paws towards her. Arati raised the scythe above her head to strike.

The tigress snarled. She wrinkled her mouth and bared her teeth. Arati almost dropped the scythe in fright but held her ground.

The two stared at each other. A sound from her son's room made Arati turn around. In a flash, the tigress grabbed a bleating goat and plunged into the water. Arati opened her mouth to raise the alarm.

Sheeba turned around with the goat held between her teeth. She knew she was taking a risk because if people came running at the woman's call, she would have to leave her prey and escape.

Arati, however, did not shout. She just stood with her mouth gaping, the semi-circular blade of the scythe gleaming in the moonlight. This surprised Sheeba. She wondered why the woman was not raising the alert. They all did. Sheeba stood watchful, her amber eyes boring into the woman's white ones.

Arati stood dazed. Why was she not able to shout for help? Was she paralyzed with fear? Strangely she felt perfectly calm. She could see the animal's body throbbing in anticipation of her next move. Her huge chest was heaving beneath the listless body of the goat that she still held between her teeth. This probably was her only meal of the day.

Arati knew what hunger was. In the aftermath of the cyclone, there were days and nights when she had gone without food. The nausea resulting from the rumblings of her empty stomach was unbearable. But she had still gone foraging for food for her son.

Suddenly, something clicked inside her. She knew she was not looking at a beast to be feared, but at a mother who, like her, had risked everything to forage for her family. Arati slowly lowered the scythe and stood watching as Sheeba sank into the water and swam away with her meal gripped between her teeth, glad that she had won the battle tonight.

Tomorrow, however, would be another struggle and Sheeba knew she may not always be the victor!

Amrita Chatterjee lives and works in India. She has published short stories and travel stories in magazines and on travel websites. She self-published her first novel, *Hiraeth – where the heart belongs* on Amazon. Both the print and e-book versions are available on all Amazon marketplaces. It has been widely appreciated and reviewed by many of her readers. She is passionate about storytelling. She has created a story loom on her blog amritawrites.com where she weaves stories drawn from life around her.

HARMONY HALL

Chad Crossley

The world will turn, he decided there that night. *Whether you turn with it or against it, the world still turns.*

He held her hand tightly in his, tightly because he knew that which she could not. He was not afraid. No, it wasn't fear he felt as he sat there on that warm night in June. It was something different, something more tangible.

He held her hand, looking down at her fingers so deftly intertwined within his own. He could feel the nervousness in her grip. He pulled her closer to him.

"What do you think it is?" she asked.

He did not answer her.

The silence of the evening enveloped them, that interloper challenged only by the steady, rhythmic creaking of the wooden porch under the weight of their chairs. He didn't have to look up. He saw her staring far off into the distance; yet, he only stared at her.

He had loved this woman since the moment he first saw her. She was the light in his life, the light guiding him through the darkness that had overtaken much of what he knew. For these were, after all, dark times.

It was 1929 as August Claus Rohweder sat there on that porch with the woman he hoped to one day marry. It was on this particular night, the third night in a row in fact, that he had come to sit with Florence at her home.

Florence hardly minded this. To her, Gus, as she so fondly referred to him, was the finest man in all of Grand Island, maybe even all of Nebraska. She did, however, notice the nervous energy within him these past few days, the tint of worry in his eyes. She knew Gus would never divulge. Admittedly, he had always been a man of few words. It wasn't just the hard times lately either. He was a strong man, like the men of the olden days—resolute and unbending. He busied himself with work, finding solace in the fact that he still had a job at all. Florence knew how he felt, even if he did not show it. Like the rest of the country, he had to be worried; he must be—but this was something different.

As the darkness grew, Gus sat there and wondered what Florence thought of it all. He felt lucky—to have her, a job, to be where he was. He wondered just how bad things really were. "The Great Depression," as the papers were now calling it, was something never before seen. Within his own private thoughts he explained it as something sensationalized to instill fear. How *great* could it really be? This was America after all, the civilized and industrial powerhouse of the world. Could such a goliath really fall?

Gus tried to not think of such things. What good would thinking do anyway? He was but one man, a simple butcher in a simple town, tucked away within the corn fields and farmlands of America's interior. His opinions mattered little. Leave it to the government, to the leaders, he would often say. Such matters could not be fixed by ordinary men.

This particular thought was on his mind as he walked back to his small home just three days ago. With the sweat of his labors on his brow and his dried and bloody apron in hand, Gus paused, unexpectedly, as an old friend approached.

"Hey there, Gus! Heading home now, are ya?"

"Sure am, Pete . . . been a long day," Gus replied.

"I bet, I bet. Say, how would ya feel 'bout coming with me and the boys to the hall tonight?"

Gus peered down at his feet as he shuffled his left boot in the dusty road. "I dunno, Pete, I mean—it's been a long day and all . . ."

"Oh come on," he pleaded, "It'll be fun, I promise. There's a group in town. They're givin' a speech and everything. The guys haven't seen you in ages, Gus. I promise it'll be a good time."

Gus shifted his weight to his right side and looked into Pete's eyes with a growing grin.

"Everyone will be there," Pete chimed in wilily.

"Alright then, I suppose I could stop in for a bit," Gus said as the two men shook hands.

Later that evening, around eight or so, Gus met up with Pete and the group. He recognized the others immediately, despite their messy clothes and unshaven faces. Jim, Robert, and John were there along with Pete. They all said their hellos and set off for the hall.

Gus had only been a couple of times: once with his brother, years ago, and once when he took Florence there on a date. Harmony Hall was the best Grand Island had to offer. Dancing, music, and fun were assured—the hall sat as the place where everyone went for a good escape from the mundane. Gus decided that maybe this wasn't such a bad idea. Perhaps he could take his mind off of his worries for a night; perhaps he too would even have some fun.

As they approached the hall, Gus noticed the bright, enamel-like, white paint coating its wooden walls. Built within an old barn, it resembled a place quite familiar—a place at home within the acres and acres of cornfields.

The men had arrived just in time as the music slowly quieted and the speaker for the evening approached the stage. He was a man of distinguished looks, Gus thought. There he stood, a man in a suit—not a rag-tagged suit like Gus' own, but a proper one. This man was a man of means, a man of money and, by the way he stood there at the center of attention, a man of conviction. He commanded the attention of those people gathered there that night, his presence inescapably compelling. Gus looked around the room. He realized he knew nearly everyone in attendance. Mr. and Mrs. Johnston, the Meyer brothers, and even Hank from the post office right down the street from his own butcher shop. Gus felt content there in that room, feeling for the first time in a long while that the troubles of his life, even the troubles of the nation as a whole, could, for the moment, wait.

"I come to you, my friends," the man began, "in a time of turmoil and necessity."

Gus and the room at large grew silent.

"It is because of such dark times that I am here, with you, to decide our fates. We must act, my brothers and sisters, and act we shall! The time for fear is over, the time for worry is past. Our actions cannot be defined by such means. We must rise up, together, and reclaim what is ours!"

Gus looked around him, looked at Pete and the others, and saw the captivating pull of this man, the sway he held over those assembled there in that room. He saw the longing to believe this man's words in their eyes, the desire to commit their lives to such a message. It was palpable, simply and wholly.

"It is our due right for us to stand together," the man continued, "and unite under our shared link! We have rid our homes of this perversion, rid our neighborhoods of the impure and sinful, rid our communities of that which is not us; and, for that, I commend you, my friends! But still, we have a threat amongst us! Still, we have work to do!"

Gus felt a sense of uneasiness within as the rest of the room erupted with a crash of applause and cheers.

Suddenly, men clad in white robes entered through the doors of the hall, their faces uncovered, smiling as though they knew they were in a home of their own.

"We must ensure the survival of the white Protestant," the man boomed, "and his children, and grandchildren after him! We must continue the work of our fathers before us. It is essential to keep out the Negro, the Homosexual, the Jew, Gypsy, and Chinaman! We must ensure this land, our land and home, as the haven for those like us. We must sustain the Klan, our Klan, and its messages at all costs, my brothers! It is for the survival of the bloodline of our race that we must endure!"

Gus felt lost in the room, drowned out by the noise of such ardent support from the men and women he knew as his neighbors. He felt sick and, much worse, afraid.

"It is for this goal that I am now here before you," the orator exclaimed. "This community here in the heart of mighty Nebraska is now directly threatened by the Papist menace! In fact, it is that Catholic Church, that abomination of St. Michaels just in the center of town down on your very own Sixth Street, which stands as the center for such corruption. It has been brought to my attention that they have amassed an arsenal of weapons within their basement, and, even more startling my friends, they seek to use it as a means of infecting our children with their damnable scripture by force! We cannot accept this direct and blatant attack on our lives, brothers and sisters! No, we must act!"

It was then that Gus felt he must leave, that he needed to escape, needed it as much as he needed air.

He inwardly knew that they must know—that, surely, they must have known.

Florence and her family were Catholic. Christ, Gus himself had even committed to the idea of converting in order to marry her. He had been to that Church himself, had even been in the basement! Not even one week ago he had seen the basement himself—he, with his own two eyes. There were no weapons; there wasn't anything at all except chairs and old dusty bibles. The whole thing was a farce, preposterous as it was sad.

Gus went straight to Florence's house that evening, three nights ago, and sat there, much like he did tonight on that same porch. He did not know what to expect. He was fearful of whether the Klan would act, or, more importantly, against whom. He knew one thing for certain; he knew he must keep Florence safe.

He chuckled to himself, secretly and without explanation. He thought back to that night and back to Harmony Hall—the very name seemed like a bad punch line to an even worse joke. He realized there and then that harmony and hatred walk hand in hand, forever linked in the hearts of men—and that too saddened him.

He looked at her and smiled.

He held her hand tightly in his, tightly because he knew that which she could not. He was not afraid. No, it wasn't fear he felt as he sat there on that warm night in June. It was something different, something more tangible.

He held her hand, looking down at her fingers so deftly intertwined within his own. He could feel the nervousness in her grip. He pulled her closer to him.

"What do you think it is?" she asked.

He did not answer her.

He knew what it was.

As they sat there together that night, in the hill-less countryside that only Nebraska could offer, they saw the fire far off in the distance.

Gus looked at Florence as he held her close to him. He placed his hand gently on her cheek and guided her face up towards his.

He kissed her sweetly with all the love he had in him to give. He kissed her and hid her gaze from the monstrosity burning there, far off near her very own church.

It was an effigy of hate he decided—a cross symbolic of Christ's love burning in the flames of all man's ignorance.

"What do you think it is," she asked him once more.

"I haven't the slightest idea," he answered, holding her tight.

Chad Crossley received his MFA in fiction from Chapman University. Firmly believing in the transcendent power of words, he strives to write meaningful works that reflect the voice of the individual in their uniquely personal space in time. His work may be found within the pages of *East Jasmine Review*, *Mojave River Review*, *Ghost City Press*, *Spiral Orb*, and elsewhere. He is currently living in Portland, Oregon, and working on a new novel.

CHILDREN'S STORIES

ALYSSUM'S WISH

Daniel Ice

A long time ago, there was a girl named Alyssum who lived in a small village. The village was nestled in a dense forest, and Alyssum was surrounded by friends and free time. Her favorite pastime was to pick flowers from the wild gardens in the woods, and nothing compared to the joy she had when she would scavenge for the most beautiful blooms she could find.

But there was one time of year when she could not pick flowers. In the throes of winter, the flowers would be crushed by the snow and cold. She hated winter for killing her flowers every year, and, as her friends played in the fluffy blankets of snow, she would sit inside her family's cozy cottage and scowl.

She knew she couldn't stop winter from coming and destroying her flowers every year. Her mother would tell her that it was just how the world worked, but she couldn't live at ease with it when her flowers so desperately needed her help.

One day in the middle of a particularly nasty winter, Alyssum's friends went to visit her and asked her to come outside to play.

"I don't want to," she said, snuggling closer to the fire.

"Is this about those flowers again? You're being ridiculous," her friends said, starting to laugh, "Why do you care if they die at all? They come back every year."

They did come back every year despite the bitter cold, but it was seeing the life drained from them and their wilting away to nothing that made her so depressed. She wasn't sure why, but seeing flowers with no life left in them always made her eyes water.

She dealt with enough teasing from her friends that day. Later that afternoon, determination got the better of her, and she set off on a quest to get rid of winter once and for all.

She journeyed into the woods, frowning as her breath puffed like a cloud in the cold air, wishing with all her might that the snow would disappear. She kicked at the snow, willing it to melt as she wandered further into the forest and continued to think of something that might get rid of winter forever.

She wandered for what seemed like a long time when she saw a woman in the distance. She wore a heavy green coat and her hair shone like the night, though it was day. Her face was pale, and her cheeks were bitten raw by the cold, but she was smiling. Alyssum strode toward the woman, looked up at her, and demanded to know how she could be smiling despite the winter weather.

"You have much to learn, young one," the woman said with a hearty chuckle, "winter has its wonders."

"But winter kills all the flowers every year," Alyssum said sadly. "I wish winter would go away so I don't have to watch them die."

"That is quite a wish, but it is what you truly desire?"

Alyssum nodded impatiently.

"Young lady, I happen to know how to grant wishes. Would you like me to grant you one?"

Alyssum's eyes widened and her breath caught in her throat. This was just what she was yearning for!

"Yes! I would be so grateful!"

"A wish simply doesn't come to you," the woman said. "I must have the proper ingredients. I need you to bring me three things. Bring me something that hangs upside down but does not have hands or feet."

Alyssum narrowed her eyes at the woman, thinking long and hard about what she could be talking about.

"Take a walk through the winter woods and you will find what I ask for."

Alyssum set off immediately, her eyes vigilant and watchful for any sign of what she might need. She thought and thought, but no matter how far she walked and thought, she could not think of the answer to the mysterious riddle.

"If only making wishes weren't so hard," Alyssum said sourly.

At that moment, she felt a drop of water fall on her head.

She looked up and another cold droplet landed on her eye.

"For heaven's sake!" she shouted as she took a step back, staring at a low hanging branch and at the water-dropping culprit.

There was an icicle above, slowly dripping water.

For a moment, she smiled at her silliness, but her mouth set again into a firm line and her eyes narrowed.

Something that hangs upside down but has no hands or feet.

She readied herself under the branch, then leaped into the air to grasp it in her hand, breaking it away from its wooden perch. She looked at it and though she felt the cold through her mittens, she saw something that made her laugh. Her reflection was quite long, and she laughed at how her nose seemed to droop in such a funny way.

She stared at it and made faces at the icicle all the way back to the woman.

"I see you've found the first ingredient. What a clever girl you are," she said, "but there are two more that remain. Now, I need you to bring me something that glitters like starlight but is on the ground."

Alyssum was intrigued by this riddle and set off in another direction. She looked down at the ground, but only saw fluffy snow. Every now and again she would spot a branch or a bush or blade of grass clinging to life, but nothing that glittered. She kicked up the snow as high as she could and listened to the crunching beneath her as she walked.

She wove through tree trunks and branches, unsure of where to go next until she spotted a ray of sunlight in the distance. She wondered if that's what the woman could have meant, but sunlight was impossible to catch.

She picked up her pace until she reached a clearing in the trees and she gasped at what she saw.

In the gap between the trees, the sunlight landed on the snow and made it sparkle like diamonds. Alyssum was frozen on the spot, not feeling the cold hugging her arms and legs. She stared into the shimmery sea of snow and realized this was what the woman needed.

She tried to grab the snow, but it fell apart in her hands. She felt panic rising in her stomach, unsure of how to carry this sparkling snow, but then she remembered what her friends would do this time of year. She rolled a patch of snow in her hands, making a beautiful snowball. Rather pleased with herself, she turned to walk back into the woods but stopped when she saw the woman watching her from a distance.

"I've got the second ingredient!" Alyssum said, showing her the glittering snowball.

"Wonderful!" the woman said, walking toward her.

The woman took the snowball, putting it into her coat pocket. Alyssum wondered if it wouldn't melt in her coat, but she said nothing.

"What's the last thing I need to get?" Alyssum asked, having so much fun on this scavenger hunt, just like she would when she scavenged for the best flowers.

"Lastly, I need you to bring me something that bleeds red but is not dying."

Alyssum felt that the last two riddles were much easier than this one. She was completely unsure of where to go.

"Why don't you go where you love to go when it isn't winter? Go to where you pick flowers, you may find what you need there."

Without another word, Alyssum ran through the woods to her favorite picking spot, toward home. She drank in the cold as she ran, grateful that it was cooling her from her exercise. Once she reached her favorite spot, that familiar cold feeling of sadness seeped into her bones. There were no flowers here. Nothing escaped the white blanket that had been placed over the green grass that was there only weeks before.

She picked up her head and tried to remain steadfast, searching everywhere for the thing that bled red but was not dying. Alyssum had hoped the woman meant something in her favorite place had survived, but not a flower could be found.

She stepped forward and heard a different sound beneath her, not so much a crunch as a squelch.

She picked up her shoe and saw that her foot was covered in a red goo. She looked in the snow and discovered what remained of a small red ball, but she couldn't put a name to what she had stepped on.

She looked ahead into a green bush covered with snow and spotted a dot of the color red. She walked closer and examined the small speck. She brushed the snow away and saw a small, red berry.

"Holly berries!" Alyssum exclaimed with joy and picked a lone berry from its nest in the bushes, recognizing that she had stepped on a berry. "I've found everything I need for my wish!"

"Yes, you have," said the voice of the woman.

Alyssum turned to see the woman and hurriedly gave her the berry.

"Now we have all the ingredients for your wish, and here is where I must apologize to you. I could have granted your wish as soon as you had asked."

"Then why didn't you?" Alyssum said, crossing her arms in a pout.

"I wanted you to know what you were asking for. You were asking for no more icicles to make faces into, no more snow to play in and admire in the sunshine, and no more discovering that some plants do survive this time of year. Winter is one of the most magical times of the year. Just as your flowers are beautiful, so are many other things in life."

Alyssum looked around at the snow, took a bracing breath of cool air, and sighed. As much as she did not want to admit it, she was growing fond of walking through the snow and was wondering what other winter things she had been missing out on.

"You have a noble heart, Alyssum. You wanted to wish away winter because it caused your flowers to wilt and die. Because of this, I will grant you a wish, but think very carefully about what you would wish for."

Alyssum recalled the small joys she had as she roamed through the wintery woods, and she knew instantly what she wanted most in her heart.

"I wish that there was a flower that would bloom every year to remind me that winter is beautiful, just like my flowers are."

The woman smiled broadly and said, "When spring comes next year and for every year until the end of time, you will see a flower that blossoms a myriad of white blooms, and these flowers will be called Sweet Alyssum."

For the next several days, Alyssum questioned herself about whether she had truly met with a mystery woman, after she told the story to her mother. Her mother said she'd never met someone like this woman in her life. None of her friends had met her either, but they didn't tease her about it when she agreed to throw snowballs with them.

That next spring, Alyssum was curious to see if her wish came true. She went out on a walk alone to the berry grove where she had found the holly berries and smiled her biggest smile when she saw on the ground a blanket of white covering the ground, a blanket of small white blooms that looked like snow.

Danielle Ice dreamed of writing and one day publishing her books ever since she was in elementary school and won a writing contest with her story about fairies that live in pumpkins around Halloween (very on-brand for a seven-year-old). From there, she practiced writing novels and short stories mostly in the science fiction/fantasy genre.

She loves movies, video games, going on obscenely long walks, music, writing books, and people reading her books! And her husband. But only slightly more than her cat.

A Very Beautiful Rainbow

Marcus Mulenga

Once upon a time, up in the great big sky, there lived a very beautiful thing named Roy. No one knew what kind of thing he was, not even himself. He was made up of seven lovely colors: a radiant red, a fiery orange, a glistening yellow, a lush green, a deep blue, a dark indigo, and a brilliant violet. Roy was by far the most beautiful thing anyone had ever seen!

On one particular day, Roy decided to take a walk through a valley that was full of gray flowers. In fact, everything except for Roy was dull and colorless. After a while, Roy came upon a gray rose named Riley. At once, she said to Roy, "I don't believe my eyes! You are the most beautiful thing I've ever seen! Could you please share just one of your colors with me?" At first, Roy hesitated. He loved all of his colors very much. But he knew that if he gave up one of them, he would still have six left.

And with that, Riley became a radiant red rose. Her gray was gone forever!

Roy continued on his stroll, and eventually he found himself on a forest trail. There, he met a gray butterfly named Amelia. The instant she caught sight of him, she exclaimed, "What a sight to see! You are the most beautiful thing I've ever seen! Can you please share just one of your colors with me?" Roy thought long and hard about this. He reasoned that he could spare to share just one more color.

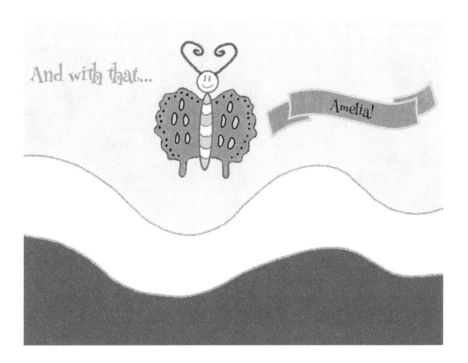

And with that, Amelia became a fiery orange butterfly. Her gray was gone forever!

"Wow!"

As Roy finished up his leisurely walk, he decided to look up at the clouds. That's when he noticed the gray sun, Iggy. "Wow!" Iggy cried out right away. "You are the most beautiful thing I've ever seen! Would you please share just one of your colors with me?" Roy was beginning to feel very anxious about giving away so many of his colors. Then he decided to do some math in his head. If he had started out with seven colors . . . and he had given away three of them . . . then he would have four colors left, which was still plenty of colors. That helped to put his mind at ease.

And with that, Iggy became a glistening yellow sun. His gray was gone forever!

After he was done looking up at the clouds, Roy next looked down at the ground and noticed that he was standing in the midst of a gray field of grass named Nelson, who said to him, "My, my! You are the most beautiful thing I've ever seen! Will you please share just one of your colors with me?" Everything was happening so quickly that Roy had forgotten the number of colors he had left! Had he given away three of them, and had four left? Or had he given away four of them, and had three left? He couldn't remember, so he decided to give up just one more color, and afterwards he would sit down and count out loud how many he had left.

And with that, Nelson became a lush green field of grass. His gray was gone forever!

After finding a place to sit down and carefully count out his remaining colors, Roy realized that he had just three left! Right at that moment, Roy looked across from where he was sitting and met the gaze of Baylor, the gray sea. Baylor took one look at Roy and shouted, "Dear waters and waves! You are the most beautiful thing I've ever seen! May you please share just one of your colors with me?" Roy didn't know what to do! He only had three of his colors left. But then he reasoned that Riley (the now radiant red rose) would probably be done with his red color by the end of the day . . . and after that he could see if Amelia was finished with his orange color . . . so why not give up his blue, just for now?

And with that...

And with that, Baylor became a deep blue sea. His gray was gone forever!

"You are the most beautiful thing I've ever seen!"

As he was beginning to make his way back to check on Riley and Amelia, Roy was suddenly approached by a tiny gray bird named Ophelia. After taking a few moments to catch her breath, she tweeted excitedly, "I'm so glad I finally caught up to you! I've been flying behind you all day long trying to reach you. I must say, you are the most beautiful thing I've ever seen! Might you please share just one of your colors with me?" For a few moments, Roy thought about this latest request. Why did everyone keep asking for his colors today? And what would happen if he had only one color left? He hadn't even checked to see if he could get any of his other colors back. Roy was about to open his mouth to say no to Ophelia . . . but then he thought about how long and how far she must have flown to come and see him. He just couldn't bear the thought of sending her flying all the way home empty-handed!

And with that, Ophelia became a dark indigo bird. Her gray was gone forever!

Now, Roy had only one color left! He got up from where he was sitting and began to run home, hoping that no one else would stop him and ask for another color along the way. But as he hurried back, he slowed down and noticed that everything around him looked very different from what he was used to seeing. First, he noticed the glistening yellow sun shining brightly over the waters of the deep blue sea. Next, he saw a fiery orange butterfly fluttering next to a radiant red rose that was in a valley of beautifully colored flowers. Finally, he saw a dark indigo bird in mid-flight over a lush green field of grass. At the beginning of his walk today, everything around Roy had been its usual dull and boring gray. But now, everything Roy looked at was just as beautiful, happy, and colorful as he was! Roy realized that by being kind and sharing his colors, he was doing a very good thing.

"Puppies aren't usually..."

The world around him was coming alive in a beautiful way! Now that he was surrounded by all these marvelous colors, Roy wanted to find someone to give his final color to! After an eager and diligent search, he at last happened upon a gray puppy named Winona. Right away, Roy said to her, "You are the grayest thing I've ever seen! I want to share my last color with you!" Before Winona could even speak up to tell him that puppies aren't usually violet, Roy did what he said he would do.

And with that, Winona became a brilliant violet puppy. Her gray was gone forever!

At this point, Roy had no more colors left to give. Finally, he made it back to his home in the great big sky. For a while, he felt glad that he had shared his colors with everyone. But then, he started to feel sad. He was no longer radiant and fiery. He was no longer glistening and lush. He was no longer deep and dark and brilliant. Now, Roy was only gray. He felt like he was no longer a very beautiful thing, and he began to miss his colors very, very much . . .

which caused Roy to cry . . .

which caused a cloud underneath him to fill up
with his tears . . .

which caused that cloud to burst open . . .

which caused it to rain . . .

which caused those falling raindrops to mix with Iggy's bright and shining sun rays . . .

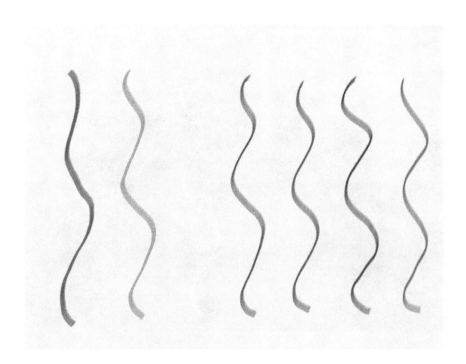

which caused those newly colored rays of light to bounce back up into the great big sky . . .

heading straight for Roy . . .

Which caused all seven of Roy's lovely colors to return back to him! He couldn't believe what had just happened! Even after giving all of his colors away, Roy had gotten them all back . . . and they looked even better than they did before! Roy learned a valuable lesson that day: it turns out that sharing what you have with others isn't just good for them; it's good for you, too! Roy used a piece of a nearby cloud to dry his remaining tears. Then he looked out and saw all of his new and colorful friends, wearing huge smiles on their faces. "Hey Roy!" they shouted up at him. "We all figured out what kind of thing you are!"

Everyone was huddled together: <u>R</u>iley, <u>A</u>melia, <u>I</u>ggy, <u>N</u>elson, <u>B</u>aylor, <u>O</u>phelia, and <u>Wi</u>nona.

"You are a RAINBOW!" And that is how Roy went from being a very beautiful thing, to being a very beautiful rainbow . . . who has very beautiful friends!

Marcus Mulenga has been reading and writing his whole life. In recent years, he has become a self-published children's author. He has several books in his creative library so far, but *A Very Beautiful Rainbow!* is his first and favorite! After reading it, you'll see why.

Any lover of fun and reading will always find delight in his colorful stories! Enjoy, and happy reading!

YOUNG ADULT

DULCE

Jessica Parrish

could feel my heart pounding inside my chest. My palms were laced with sweat and my ears were ringing. My bladder was one ache away from releasing, but I knew it wasn't time. I pressed my ear against my bedroom door although I'm not sure why. I could hear them loud and clear.

"No! Stop!" My mom's words were shrill and laced with fear. I could hear the hurt and stress in her voice. I reached my shaky hand towards my doorknob but was reluctant to turn it.

How had the night gone so sideways? Things were good at dinner. We were all laughing and having a good time. My mind raced trying to place the exact moment things went from normal, to this.

"C'mon, let's just go to bed babe. I don't want Dulce to wake up." My mom's voice was pleading now. I hated hearing the desperation in her voice. How she stayed with this horrible man, I will never know. I kept my ear pressed to the door, my hand still hovering just over the knob. I knew if I were going to make a move, it would need to be a fast one.

"You know she's wide awake," he sneered. My body shivered when he spoke. His voice was a slurred nightmare. My jaw clenched just hearing him speak. I gripped the doorknob now, a little tighter than I probably needed to, but still couldn't muster the courage to turn it.

Besides, I was only sixteen, a very petite sixteen at that. At only 4'11, I didn't stand a chance against his 6'0 tall frame.

I closed my eyes, squeezing my lids tightly. It is almost over, just stay, Dulce. Don't make it worse, I thought to myself. My bladder was screaming at me, begging for release. Damn nervous bladder. I swear I had the bladder of a Cocker Spaniel.

"NO!" My mom screamed, a blood curdling scream. There was a loud crash followed by more screams and now sobs. Without thinking, I turned the knob and nearly ripped the door off of its hinges. I ran down the hall and threw my body against my mom's bedroom door, flinging it open. I shoved past him, by him I mean her gem of a boyfriend, and laid my body on top of hers. I was determined to shield her from the next blow, or whatever was sure to come. All I knew was tonight had gone too far, she had endured enough.

"Enough!" I screeched, not even recognizing my own voice. "Just leave!" I held on tight to my mom, trying to comfort her shaking body. He mumbled a few curse words and then left the room. I waited, my body shielding hers until I heard him grab his car keys and shut the front door. Once I heard the car start up, I bolted to the front door and made sure it was locked. He has keys, I told myself, he can just come right back in.

Pushing that thought away, I ran back to my mom. She was now sitting up, but still hunched over. I knew that pose. She had a broken rib or two. "Mama?" I asked, sitting next to her on the floor. "Mom, are you ok?" I did my best to sound strong and hide the panic in my voice.

"Sweet girl," she caressed my face, "you should have stayed in your room." Her movements caused her to wince in pain which confirmed my broken rib theory. I pulled away from her, a pained look on my face.

"Why?" I scoffed. "So he coulda killed you this time?" I stood up, feeling my blood boil, but knowing that it was mostly just adrenaline coursing through my small body.

"Baby girl, he could have hurt you," she said through gritted teeth. I watched as my mom tried to use the side of the bed to help herself stand up. She kept one hand clutched to her side and winced in pain. Yep, broken rib. Called it.

"Mom," I pleaded with her, now helping her stand the rest of the way, "I'm calling the cops, getting you an ambulance, and we're taking you to the hospital."

Her eyes went wide, and she shook her head no. "No ambulance," she said, her jaw clenching so tight I worried her teeth would break. "No cops." I watched her in disbelief. How could this beautiful, logical, sensible woman let some monster beat her night after night? She was my whole world. Could she not see how much more she deserved?

"Well, I'm calling someone. Your ribs are broken, and you need to go to the hospital." I angrily grabbed her cell phone from the nightstand and began searching her contacts.

"Call Aunt Wendy, she'll know what to do." My mom sat on the edge of her bed with her eyes closed. She already had the faint hint of a black eye. Oddly enough, that bruise rising on her cheek was enough for me to lose my battle with composure. Seeing my mom's beautiful face swollen and bruised, shattered my heart. He had never hit her in the face before.

"Aunt Wendy?" I spoke into the phone, my voice trembling and shaking, "It's Dulce."

There was a momentary pause on the other line. It was already past one in the morning, to be fair. "Dulce?" she asked in a panicked tone. "Your mom?" Her voice broke. That caused me to shatter into a million pieces. I knew that fear in her voice. She was wondering if I was calling to tell her my mom was dead.

"Mom's fine, Aunt Wendy." Lie, my brain screamed at me. "Well, not fine, but she will be. Can you come over?" My words were a slew of sobs and hiccups. "Tonight was bad." I couldn't stop shaking.

"Sweet girl," she breathed a sigh of relief and then she was back on the line. "Is he still there?"

"No." I cried harder, suddenly realizing that he could come back at any moment. "Good. I'm on my way. Hand the phone to your mom, baby girl. I will keep her talking until I get there." She gave me a few other instructions, things to keep me busy. She instructed me to lock all the doors and windows and I was to tell her immediately if he came back. She also told me to gather an overnight bag for my mom and me, as we were going to stay the rest of the weekend at her house.

Once I handed the phone to my mom, I hurried to the hallway bathroom. I barely made it on time to release my poor strained bladder. Sweet relief, I thought. After that was handled, I scurried to my room and packed way too much for just one night. Wishful thinking, I guess. I reached for my makeup bag and my hair straightener and then headed back to mom's room to pack her things.

I stopped approaching when I heard her crying on the phone to Aunt Wendy. "His eyes were black, Wendy," she whispered. "Like he wasn't even there." I stayed put, not wanting to be nosey, just giving her some space to confide in her best friend, whom I dubbed my aunt. "He wasn't going to stop, Wendy." More sobs. "He said he wouldn't stop until . . . until . . ." she broke down crying even harder this time, now verbalizing her pain with each sob. "I know, I know. You're right. This is the last time."

She sounded sure enough, but I knew that too was just wishful thinking. I walked into the room, acting like I wasn't paying attention to her conversation. There were mostly just one-word answers now and I knew that was on my behalf. I grabbed some sweats, yoga pants, and several shirts for her and threw them in my bag. I went to her bathroom to grab some of her things and then gasped.

I dropped the duffle bag and nearly dropped to the floor. There was blood all over the counter and floor. I turned to look at my mom and saw that her nose was shifted drastically to the left. Why had I not seen that before? Her eyes met mine, and the look of pure shame that was emanating from her gaze made my throat dry.

Instead of yelling at her more, I quietly grabbed a towel and began cleaning up the blood, her blood, from the counter, floor and walls. I sobbed as I scrubbed my mom's blood from the white tile floors, vowing to myself that I would do everything in my power to make sure that a man never laid a finger on her again.

Just as I was about finished, I heard a car pull into our driveway. "Mama, he's back!" I whimpered, upset with myself at how cowardly I sounded. My heart skipped several beats and I stood up and ran to her, still clutching that blood-soaked towel. My eyes were wild, and I was preparing, mentally, for our escape.

"No sweet girl, shhh," my mom's voice soothed me. "It's Aunt Wendy. Go to the door, let her in." Her words took a second to sink in, but once they did, I bolted for the front door. Even though I knew it was my aunt coming to save us, I still checked the peep hole, making sure that it was, in fact, her.

"It's me Dulce, it's ok love." she said through the closed door. Her voice sounded like music to my ears. Sweet relief, I thought.

I unlocked the door and only opened it enough for her to squeeze her slender body through, almost fearing that he might be hiding behind her and try to push his way in. She wrapped her unnaturally long arms around my tiny body and pulled me into a bear hug.

"My sweet girl," she kissed the top of my head. "You did so good tonight." She placed her hands on my shoulders and looked down at me and the bloody towel that I was still holding onto for dear life. I watched her swallow her emotions as her composure faltered, but only momentarily. "Your mom told me how you saved her life." She smiled although there was sorrow written all over her face.

Saved her life, I heard my inner voice say, reassuring me. I held on tightly to Aunt Wendy and let my tears flow freely. We walked hand in hand to my moms' room . . . me, still holding that bloody towel. "Why don't you throw that in the wash, sweet girl? I'll gather up your mom and then we'll go." She smiled that gorgeous smile at me and then left my side to tend to my mom. I tossed the towel in the trash and ran back to the room to get the overnight bag. Aunt Wendy and I guided my mom through the house and out the door.

Once the fresh night air hit my tear-stained face, I was able to breathe—like actually breathe. Wendy helped her into her car and then helped me with the bag. I sat in the back with my mom, holding her hand as we drove to the hospital. Wendy had convinced her that she not only needed to be seen, but that this needed to be reported. I rubbed the back of my mom's hand as we drove through the city, the lights illuminating the car as we passed. I looked up occasionally to meet Aunt Wendy's eyes in the rearview mirror. Her gaze was trained on me and my mom. I don't think she looked at the road once that night.

··◆◆◆◆◆··

It had only taken three weeks this time. Three weeks and he was back. I stood there, in complete shock. No way this was happening. "Mom," I begged, my eyes filling to the brim with tears. Don't cry, I screamed in my head. Hold them in. He doesn't get to see those tears fall.

"Sweet girl," she sighed heavily, trying to untwist her hand from his. My jaw clenched as I watched the subtle movement of his knuckles turning white as he squeezed her hand tighter, keeping her from reaching out to me. And she didn't resist.

My heart froze. That right there, that one gesture, told me everything that I needed to know. She chose him. I tried to breathe, my lungs feeling like they couldn't inflate enough to keep me alive. She chose him. Not you. This will never stop. He will never leave.

"Mom?" I tried once more, needing her to respond to me. To stand up for herself. To stand up for me. But she didn't move. She didn't speak. She just stood there, already a ghost of the mom that I had this morning.

I was done. I was done hearing him. Done looking at him. Done letting him back into our lives. She didn't choose you, that shattered voice inside my head told me again. That last thought was the fuel I needed. I pushed through, sprinting full force toward them, ducking my tiny frame under their entwined hands. I shoved them both aside with some superhuman strength and I ran out the door.

I ran straight down the driveway and veered to the right, not knowing where I was going. All I knew was I needed to leave. I had to get away. My legs pumped harder and harder. My lungs began to ache and burn from the lack of oxygen that wouldn't pass through. My vision blurred as my tears poured from my eyes. I must have looked like a lunatic, running down the street, crying and flailing, but I didn't care. I needed to get somewhere safe, somewhere far away. Away from *Him*. And away from Her.

She might have chosen Him, but I choose better. This cycle, this nightmare, this family curse will end with me. Even if that means I have to go at it alone.

Author Jessica Parrish makes her debut publication with "Dulce," a young adult short story that placed second in its genre in SOOP's Short Story Anthology Writing Contest. A self-proclaimed trauma fiction writer, Jessica pulls from her own experiences and writes about real, gritty topics in ways that are raw and relatable. Fairy tales and happily ever afters are not always evident, but sometimes just surviving is the true victory. She is an up-and-coming author with plans to release original pieces in many different genres, ranging from adult fiction to children's books, and everywhere in between. She wholeheartedly believes that there is healing in sharing, which is what she aims to do with her stories.

THE COLLECTOR

Haley Forté

Every town has an urban legend.

When it came to Rosalind's, this story was much more than a piece of fiction. Every year, on the same weekend in October, the carnival would roll into town with its colorful lights, oddly dressed characters, and the feeling that something was about to change. Families flocked to the fairgrounds to play games, ride rickety attractions, and escape from reality for a few hours. Since the carnival first appeared thirty years before, Roz had never quite liked one specific tent that was always tucked away in the back of the red and white labyrinth.

This tent didn't have any signs that let patrons know what, or *who*, was behind its veiled entrance, but one thing always remained: people went in, but not everyone came out. Roz always thought it was because of a hidden back door or perhaps it led to another tent nearby, but whenever she walked past it, a chill would cascade down her spine as if it were midwinter rather than the start of autumn. It was as if the air that surrounded the tent was significantly colder than the rest of the world.

There was a rumor behind the odd carnival attraction, one that was meant to scare kids and make them double-check their closets and under their beds before going to sleep at night. It was the tale of The Collector. Nobody knew what he looked like and the story said that even those that ventured into his dwelling could never remember if they saw him there at all. It was the biggest mystery in the farming town, but one Rosalind was determined to solve that October weekend.

"This is a bad idea," Mason said as he stared up at the entrance to the tent. A slight breeze ruffled the thick fabric, only adding to the dread that settled in his stomach. Bells and whistles echoed around the kids as they held their tickets tight in their hands. "Please tell me I am not the only one who thinks this is a *bad idea.*"

"Lots of people have done it," Olivia reasoned, her voice uncertain. Her hands twisted into her blonde hair as she shuffled straw with the toes of her new Reebok sneakers.

"Don't tell me you're afraid of a legend," Roz teased, facing her two best friends.

"Legends are *meant* to make people afraid, Roz!" Mason exclaimed. "Bigfoot? Loch Ness? The Boogie Man!"

"I'm not sure you can classify that last one as a legend," Roz said.

"I still don't like it," Mason mumbled, shifting on his feet. He had been roped into joining the girls on what Olivia was calling their "ghost hunt." Mason was usually the one to follow them when it came to their adventures. Whether it was running through Farmer Greg's cornfield or liberating the frogs in the high school science lab, he was always on board. However, this was nearly crossing the line of stupidity, even for them.

"You could always stay outside," Olivia offered as she began walking towards the tent, a teasing smile on her face. Roz followed her and then with a scoff, Mason jogged to catch up with them.

"Just don't leave me alone," he said, and then Olivia reached back and looped her arm through his.

"Okay, Velma, don't worry, I got you," she teased.

"Why is Mason, *Velma*?" Roz asked as they pushed through the curtains and into the main tent. Before Olivia could answer, they froze. The tent, while it looked small from the outside, was much more vast than they had anticipated. It was as if someone had shoved an entire hay maze into a large canvas bubble.

"We should have brought backup," Mason whimpered.

"We *are* the backup," Roz corrected and then took Mason's other arm. From where the three kids stood, they couldn't see anyone else. "Come on."

The three of them moved into the maze, their eyes scanning for traps or clowns that would pop out, but nothing came from the hay bales that made up the walls. Their breath was visible in front of them which would have been normal for October in the Midwest, but as they moved further into the maze, the temperature seemed to drop even lower.

Suddenly, the lights flickered above them and the walls seemed to move toward them from the side. "Run?" Olivia asked, her confidence slowly leaving.

"Good idea," Roz agreed as she took off at a sprint, her best friends trailing after her. Roz kept running until there were no more turns and when she stopped, she was met with a single archway. A neon sign above it read "EXIT." Sighing in relief, she turned around only to find that Mason and Olivia were nowhere to be seen. "Guys?" Roz whispered, but there was no response.

Getting nervous, Roz backed up until she walked through the small entrance. As her feet shuffled across the straw-covered floor, she began to slide as ice crystals formed beneath her feet. Roz glanced up and stumbled as she beheld what was in front of her.

Or rather who.

A tall man in a white coat with white hair stared at her with a smile on his pale, gaunt face. Roz gulped as she looked at the odd man. When his grin widened, rows of pointy teeth slid out from his gums. Roz turned to run, but slipped, hitting the floor with a thud. Disoriented, she tried to get to her feet, but everything around her was too white and too cold. The last thing she heard was someone calling her name.

·•✦◆✦•·

When Rosalind came to, she was sitting outside of a nearby stand with a blanket wrapped around her shoulders.

"You need to drink something," a voice came from her right. Blinking a few times, she turned her head to see Mason sitting next to her, a bottle of water in his hands.

"What happened?" Roz asked, taking the drink.

"I guess the maze was scarier than we first thought. We got separated and then I think you fell and hit your head. I found you and helped you outside. Looks like I wasn't *Velma* after all but rather Fred," Mason said with a grin, feeling quite proud of himself. Roz shrugged off the blanket and looked around, scanning the crowd.

"Where's Olivia?" Roz wondered.

"Who?" Mason asked. Roz looked at him, confused.

"Olivia," Roz repeated, "she was with us when we went into the tent." Mason shook his head.

"Roz, nobody else was with us," he said slowly. "How hard did you hit your head?" Mason laughed as he sank back down next to her, glad to be out of the shuddersome tent. Still, Rosalind couldn't shake the feeling that there *had* been someone else with them. She had told both of them to run, but then she couldn't remember anything else after that.

Olivia was there though, wasn't she?

··✦✦✦✦✦··

In the dim light of the unmarked tent, a tall man in a white coat with white hair walked the maze with a small globe balanced in his hands.

As he strode through the straw labyrinth, a tiny sound echoed from the prize he held. A rhythmic tapping reached his ears and he smiled, listening to the familiar sound. Taking the last few turns, the man entered the back section of the tent, the temperature was well-below freezing, exactly the way he liked it.

Placing the globe on a nearby table, he began to pack up his things as the weekend in October was coming to a close. As he worked, the tapping became louder and more frequent. Calmly, the tall man walked over to the table and lifted the globe to his eye. "Do not worry," he whispered as an icy breath blew over the glass, "you are not going to be alone much longer." Behind the crystal ball, a young girl pounded her tiny fists on the wall of her new prison. A young girl with blonde hair and new Reebok sneakers.

The tall man smiled wide, showing his pointed teeth and she fell back, landing in the white powder beneath her feet. With a laugh, he swirled the globe around, causing the fake snow to form a contained blizzard around the girl who was once known as Olivia James. "Let me out!" she screamed, fighting through the snow, but the tall man simply laughed and walked over to a bare shelf.

"You have made a lovely addition to my collection," he said as he placed the globe on its brand-new brass stand. The tall man admired his newest prize and then turned away, disappearing back into the main tent.

Breaking through the false snowstorm, Olivia pressed her nose to the glass before her and screamed at what she saw. Rows and rows of shelves were lined with custom snow globes and in each one, small figures banged their tiny fists against the glass. Their screams were futile and never-ending.

The Collector sees what he wants and he takes it. Nobody ever notices and nobody ever remembers it.

That is until a girl named Rosalind did.

Haley M. Forté is currently a student studying creative writing and English with a fiction concentration. Growing up in both Washington State and California, Haley has relied on her family to keep her busy and on her toes. She is a writer of many genres but prefers to sit within the realms of horror and science fiction. When she is not writing, she is curating her Star Wars helmet collection, playing apocalyptic video games, and learning all she can about the Cosmos.

SCIENCE FICTION, DYSTOPIAN & FANTASY

THE STORYTELLER'S DAUGHTER

Sophie Trist

984, fourth year of the Council of Enlightened Unity

They will hang my mother today. Despite the rain spitting from a winter sky the color of an old bruise, there is a large, festive crowd. There always is when a Storyteller is executed.

The official from the Board of Public Information, a short, gray-faced man in a gray suit and round spectacles, reads the charges into a microphone. His silver insignia, a pair of hands cupping a lit torch, winks at me like the eye of a bird of prey. Even after everything—the arrest, the trial—I still can't believe this is happening. Imagining a world without my mother is like imagining a world without the sun.

She is blindfolded when the Inquisitorial Guards lead her onto the scaffold. No one asks Rayha Igonwe if she has any last words. The torturers had cut out her tongue to keep her heretical magic locked inside.

As the executioner ties a noose around my mother's neck, her head turns this way and that, and even through the blindfold, I can feel her golden eyes searching for me, piercing me, vivisecting me. I want to run to her and vanish into thin air at the same time. I want to call out, to apologize, to . . . I don't even know.

Then, the platform drops away, and my mother's feet are swinging, swinging, swinging in the rain. Her face turns blue as her body jerks. I am overwhelmed by an urge to look away, but I keep my eyes on my mother until the hangman declares her dead. They will leave her body hanging in Pamalon's central square for three days as a reminder to other heretics. I close my eyes, knowing I can't let myself cry.

"Here, Maua, take this." My friend Anaki stands beside me as she always has, pressing a small white tablet into my hand. "It's rosedust. It'll help you forget."

I remember all of my mother's stories, treason piled on treason. I picture myself throwing Anaki's drug into the gutter. But what will that leave me with? I'm not brave like Rayha. I smile in thanks and swallow the pill dry.

971, fifth year of the Council of Serene Obedience

It was a long time before I realized that Pamalon's rulers considered my mother's stories heresy. Growing up, they were natural as breath, as much a part of me as my own heart. "We are women of the Ishva tribe, daughters of the land of Ilthasia. Our people come from far across the sea," she told me when I was five years old. My heart nearly exploded with excitement with every word she spoke.

"Ilthasia was not a land of milk and honey, but it was my home. There is so much green there, my girl, more trees and lakes than anyone in Pamalon has ever seen." As Mother spoke, the light and shadows in my tiny bedroom bent, forming the rivers and valleys and forests of Ilthasia. The air grew rich with the smells of sap and fresh leaves.

"The Ishva are children of the goddess Idessa, She Who Brings The Word. We are Storytellers, keepers of memory. My mother told me that the gift of bringing stories to life ran strong in me and my little sister Aekia," Mother continued. Images filled in my mother's story: two little dark-haired, golden-eyed girls running in the moonlight, pulling water from a well, working a loom alongside their mother, learning Storyteller magic from their father. The Ishva did not have a written language. Stories were passed down by word of mouth or in Ekati, crystal spheres enchanted to hold voices and images. Simply touch an Ekati, and the story within it comes to life in your hands.

"Can I see an Ekati, Mother?" I asked once.

Mother shook her head. "I wish you could, Maua, but all of my family's Ekati were destroyed," she told me.

"Who destroyed them?" I asked in outrage.

"Nineteen years ago, the other three tribes of Ilthasia grew jealous of our magic and united to wipe us out." These images gave me nightmares. Storytellers were drowned, burned at the stake as heretics. A girl no older than nineteen was beaten to death in a town square, her body left for the crows. Men with torches and swords raided villages, dragging men, women, and children out of their houses. They smashed Ekati that had been passed down through generations of families, destroying countless stories forever before setting everything ablaze. They killed many Ishva outright, but some, including my mother and her sister Aekia, were put in chains and marched to slave camps, where telling a story could mean death.

"I was fifteen," Mother said, her sadness too deep for tears. "They sent Aekia and me into the mines. It was so cold and dark." She shivered and rubbed at her scarred arms, and I saw a line of gaunt, hollow-eyed Ishva children herded into a dark hole, whipped bloody by stone-faced guards if quotas weren't met. I saw the brilliant Aekia, who could have become the best Storyteller in Ilthasia, wither away from illness when something from the mines got into her lungs.

"I tried everything. I sold myself to the camp guards in exchange for medicine. After working all day in the mines, I sat up with her all night, whispering all I remembered from our destroyed Ekati, telling her our stories to keep her alive. But the life just . . . drained out of her," Mother said.

I heard Aekia's final words in her own voice, preserved forever in Mother's memory. "You can't die here, Rayha. I won't be scared if I know you're free. The world doesn't want to hear about people like us, but you have to tell them." The guards had to pry my mother away from her sister's cooling body. Her screams echoed in my head for hours.

Mother told me her story over the course of weeks and months and years, the loves and dreams and deaths of my ancestors filling me until there was no room for the Maua who was trying to build a life in Pamalon.

984, fourth year of the Council of Enlightened Unity

The thick white paste burns my skin as I smear it across my face. Already, my skin is lightening, the cream bleaching the bronze hue right out of it. I smile brilliantly, hiding all traces of pain. On the outside, I'm just another dark-haired eighteen-year-old girl in a white uniform, fresh out of Upper School. Only my golden eyes, the same bright shade as my mother's, indicate that I'm a foreigner.

"Maua, we'll be late for work," Anaki calls from the main room of the tiny apartment we share with two other girls.

She's right. Thanks to the drugs I've been taking, I overslept again. I know I'm becoming addicted, but anything is better than seeing my mother's broken neck and swinging feet in my dreams. The swinging feet are somehow the worst.

Anaki and I crowd onto a packed tram that will bring us to the city center. I feel apart from everyone else. Anaki tries to engage me in our usual banter, but her voice is unusually high and tense, and when I respond with grunts and one-word answers, my friend gives up.

"You did the right thing, Maua. You know that, don't you?" Anaki asks anxiously. I nod jerkily as we get off the tram.

I work in a huge gray block that looks identical to all the other huge gray blocks lining the street. The people of Pamalon aren't known for imagination. A building that differs from its neighbors tells a story, and stories that depart from the approved narrative are not allowed. Anaki and I breeze in with a dozen other washed-out minor government bureaucrats. Most of them are young like us, girls and boys serving their internships in the year after graduation. We climb to the stairs to the third floor.

"See you at lunch," I say automatically as Anaki goes right and I go left.

My tiny cubicle is just ahead. I slow with dread when I see a stack of paperwork on my desk. Ciereth has already delivered the morning's reports. Do the Watchers ever stop?

With a resigned sigh, I sit down and pull the first form toward me. I pick up a pen and press it to the paper. But all I can see is the rainy sky, the guard tying the rope around my blindfolded mother's neck.

"Igonwe!" A sharp female voice calls my last name. I jerk to attention as my superior, Ciereth Ashtar, marches up to my desk. She's a tall, dark woman with severe, sparking eyes. "Greetings, Mistress Ashtar," I say, bending my head.

"There's work to be done," Ciereth says brusquely.

"Yes, Mistress Ashtar. I apologize for my laxity," I said. The insignia on her uniform flashes gold: a pair of hands cupping a blazing torch. My brass insignia shines dully back at her. I used to stand before the mirror and admire that badge. But now all I can see is the bonfires that burned my mother's people.

973, seventh year in the Council of Serene Obedience

"It took me several months to escape from the prison camp, but Aekia's dream kept me going. By the time I obtained the papers I needed on the black market and got a place on a ship headed for Pamalon, I knew that I was going to have you," Mother told me on my seventh birthday.

"Who was my father then?" I asked. I knew that I must have one somewhere.

"I do not speak of him, Maua. What he did to me . . . it hurts me to think about it," Mother says. Do you know what it's like, knowing that you only exist because of a man's violence? I felt dirty, as if the stain of rape was imprinted on my skin. I bathed in too-hot water in hopes of scrubbing away my unknown father's violence, my foreignness, everything that made me different.

"Do . . . do you still love me even though my father hurt you?" I asked my mother, nearly in tears.

She pulled me close. Mother always smelled of soap and baking bread and fresh summer rain. That constant fragrance was one of the many things I always loved and never understood about her. "Of course, my precious one. You gave me a reason to keep living and fighting. I almost named you Aekia, but my sister's name is too gentle for this land. Maua means One Who Suffers into Triumph. That is what I want for you, my daughter."

Mother's words brought her journey to life. The floor of our tiny apartment pitched and rolled like the deck of the rickety ship that had taken us and three hundred twenty-six other Ishva refugees across the sea. The smell of unwashed bodies crammed together in a stuffy hold filled my nose. In exchange for more rations, some of the crewmen took the younger and prettier girls into their cabins. They emerged silent, bruised, and broken.

Some of the refugees kissed the docks when they finally arrived in Pamalon, but those expecting a warm welcome were quickly disillusioned. The entry process was brutal and dehumanizing: long interrogations, invasive medical exams, derogatory comments about our filth and lack of manners whispered behind hands. Those who had managed to smuggle Ekati out of Ilthasia saw them smashed right before their eyes, a warning that our ancestors' stories were not welcome here. Mother entered the city with her dignity in tatters, but I was still growing strong and healthy inside her.

She and four other women lived in the tiny tenement apartment that had been assigned to them. They would face deportation if they did not find work within a week, so Mother took the first job she could get: scrubbing dishes at a local inn. Before I was born, two of the women who lived with Mother had married local men, another disappeared while walking home in the wee hours, and the fourth was deported for taking part in some political demonstration. Mother knew all their names, all their stories. Their ghostly forms flitted around our apartment, conjured by Mother's words. They became like aunts to me, these women preserved only by my mother's strange magic.

The stories left me burning and restless inside. I wanted things to be different, but I didn't have the faintest idea how. I couldn't name my own desires, and so I grew to hate and fear them.

My schoolmates and our teachers never questioned anything, never wondered what was beyond the boundaries we imposed on ourselves. I often got a switch on the back of my hand or across my thighs for disagreeing with my instructors or asking improper questions.

"That girl will go bad someday, mark my words. It's in her heretic blood," they whispered loud enough to make sure I heard. As the months passed, the whispers of my teachers and schoolmates drowned out my ancestors' screams, until I wanted nothing more than to become one of the crowd: nameless, faceless, voiceless, and safe.

984, fourth year in the Council of Enlightened Unity

I wish I were dead. I've thought this before, but never so clearly and powerfully as now. Light from somewhere pries at my eyelids like cruel, sharp talons. The inside of my mouth is dry and tastes like the end of the world. Where am I? This isn't the small room I share with Anaki.

I peel my gummy, crusty eyes open and see a dingy bedroom and a naked man snoring beside me. His mouth is wide open, and his breath blows his long, bushy mustache up and down, up and down. There's a paper packet half full of rosedust on the floor beside the bed, the moonlight making it glitter like broken glass.

I try to think, to remember how I got here. If I strain my brain, I come up with a vague recollection of this man guiding me out of a loud, bright tavern. Did we have sex? Our nudity indicates that we did, but just thinking about it makes my head feel like it's about to explode. After a great deal of effort, I remember what day it is. Exactly two weeks have passed since my mother's execution.

I heave myself out of bed, wait for my stomach to settle, and slip on yesterday's dirty clothes. I've got to stop this, I tell myself as I creep out of the room.

I fumble with the lock on the apartment door for a solid minute before pulling the door open. I fall more than walk down the stairs. Fortunately, the man's apartment is on the second floor. Outside, the stars are just beginning to fade, night reluctantly giving way to day. The cool air clears my head just a little, and I throw up into some convenient bushes. This makes my mouth taste even more foul, but the headache is better and I can string two thoughts together without agony.

I mean to get my bearings and head home, but my feet have other ideas. They take me into the old, horribly familiar streets of the foreign quarter, which by day rings with the sounds of people calling to one another in half a dozen discordant languages. The pushy vendors and dirty children playing in gutters are gone now. My only company is a mangy, rail-thin dog rooting through a rubbish heap. He raises his head and snarls at me as I pass. I think about kicking him but don't have the energy.

I hadn't spoken to my mother for four months before her arrest. We had gotten into a colossal argument the day I was chosen for an internship at the Board of Public Information. "You should be happy for me!" I yelled. "I've worked hard for years so I could make something of myself in Pamalon! I graduated at the top of my class! Isn't this what every mother wants for her daughter?"

I wish I could forget her response, but as I enter our old tenement through the back door (the lock broke when I was sixteen and the landlord never bothered to fix it), her words run relentlessly through my head. "You don't understand what you're doing, Maua! The Board of Public Information are monsters!"

"You're the one who doesn't understand!" I shouted back. "You're still thinking like you're in Ilthasia."

Almost before I know it, I'm standing in front of my old apartment. The lock on this door is broken too, no doubt smashed when the Inquisitorial Guards raided. I don't have to go in. No one is making me. But I need to prove to myself that I am stronger than this old place, than my regret.

I open the door carefully, remembering how I slammed it the last time, swearing I wouldn't come back until Mother apologized and accepted the way things are here. The scarred wooden table where we ate all of our meals is on its side, cracked down the middle. Pots and pans are strewn everywhere. Shattered glass crunches beneath my shoes, sounding like the bones of small children breaking.

The bedroom is in a similar state. The mattresses have been completely destroyed, covering the floor with straw. Mother's few dresses lay like tattered burial shrouds around the overturned bureau. Remarkably, the loose floorboard where Mother hid our money is still in place. Excitement and dread curdle noxiously in my stomach. Surely, the alcove must be empty.

With shaking fingers, I pull up the loose floorboard. A single sphere of black stone rests in the tiny alcove. I don't realize I've stopped breathing until my chest starts to burn. How could she have hidden this? How did the Inquisitorial Guards not find it? The fact that I know this object exists could put me on the gallows next.

When they're filled with stories, Ekati glow faintly, each Storyteller's power giving their spheres a unique hue. Mother once told me that a room full of scores of glowing Ekati was one of the most beautiful things she'd ever seen. But this Ekati is empty, waiting for me to claim the strange, forbidden magic I can even now feel singing in my blood. Mother must have known that I couldn't avoid this place forever, that my guilt would chase me back here in the end. This Ekati is her last commandment, a challenge to tell my own story.

978, fifth year in the Council of Peaceful Truth

"When and why was the Board of Public Information established?" the instructor's voice cracked through the classroom like breaking ice. I sat in the front row, as I was determined to be the very best student in the class.

Anaki raised her hand, and the teacher called on her with the slightest of approving smiles. "The Board of Public Information was founded in 727, the sixth year in the Council of Forceful Justice, in response to the Pearl Coast slave rebellion," my best (only) friend chirped.

"Exactly, Anaki. During the rebellion, the slaves used the heretical Storyteller magic to spread false propaganda to win the populace to their cause. Stories are inherently untrustworthy. They twist facts and perceptions. They pervert the way we think about ourselves and our country. How are we supposed to know what's true and what's false if information is not censored?"

A boy raised his hand, and the instructor acknowledged him. "Is this why the current council calls its reign Peaceful Truth?" he asked.

"Yes indeed, Quinden. When objectivity and truth are paramount, when we quash dangerous imaginings that would undermine the very foundation of our society, there is peace. There is no contention. Do you all know what contention means?" Most of us nodded. The few who didn't looked embarrassed and whispered to their neighbors.

My hand lifted into the air almost before I knew what I was doing. The teacher gestured for me to speak, and the rest of the class stared at me like they'd never seen a twelve-year-old girl before. "Are you saying that there's only one version of truth? Something can't be true for one person and not true for someone else?" I asked.

"That's correct, Maua. I'm glad you understand. What is true for one citizen of Pamalon is true for us all. By its very definition, the truth cannot change. It is carved into the stone of our city and into our minds." I smiled at his words, for they filled me with a huge sense of comfort and relief. They gave me what I had been looking for for years: certainty. Those words told me that I didn't have to listen to inconvenient stories. People far older and wiser than me had decided that my mother's magic was dangerous and there was only one version of truth, Truth with a capital T.

I couldn't bring Mother around to my way of thinking when I got home. She got angry when I tried to explain why I wouldn't listen to her stories anymore. "To some extent, yes, truth is objective. Rain falls from the sky. Drinking bad water makes people ill. No one with sense would deny these things. But it is also true that no matter how hard I work, we will never live in one of those fancy houses near the city center like your friend Anaki. It is also true that nearly every week, a poor woman or girl vanishes off the street, but it is never reported. It is also true that Pamalon did next to nothing while thousands of my people were being burned and worked to death in camps. The full, ungilded truth about life is rarely ever peaceful, my daughter."

"But all the legends about Idessa and the other gods and the heroine Sathia who made peace with the dragons, you know those can't be true. By telling those stories and preserving them with your magic, you know you're telling lies," I argued.

"I don't know if those stories are true or not. But even if they did not literally happen as I told you, they can teach us larger truths, truths about the world that could be. Sathia was able to stop the war between the dragons and the people of Ilthasia because she was a Storyteller. She understood that the dragons were not monsters, and she used her magic to bring that understanding, in the dragons' own voices and images, to her people. Stories can bring us closer together. Any good story should make you a little uncomfortable with the way things are." I never answered her. Though I wanted desperately to believe that Pamalon's Truth was all anyone needed, that old stories were irrelevant and even dangerous, a tiny part of me couldn't shake the feeling that Rayha Igonwe was right.

984, fourth year in the Council of Enlightened Unity

The Ekati began appearing in the early spring. People found faintly glowing crystals on street corners, on benches in public parks, on the doorsteps of their homes. When they touched the stones, they would be surrounded by the faces and voices of the city's undercaste: the teenagers who didn't qualify for Upper School and worked twelve-hour days in sweltering, unsafe factories, the parents of vanished girls, the street children reduced to stealing to survive, the immigrants and refugees victimized by slurs and attacks. The government warned people not to touch the Ekati. Pamphlets appeared in every corner of Pamalon urging citizens to let the authorities handle these dangerous objects and to report any suspicious behavior. But still, the stories spread like a quiet fire.

The Board of Public Information was frantic to find the Storyteller responsible for these "assaults on truth, unity, and the morale of our citizenry." The manhunt was covert but fierce. Spies slunk through the foreign quarter. The Council passed a law permitting "immigrants and others suspected of practicing heretical magic" to be imprisoned indefinitely without charges or trial. Ishva were arrested and interrogated at random. Most returned to their families, beaten but alive, but a few were never seen again. Some Ishva left Pamalon, deciding to take their chances back in Ilthasia. "Fools, all of them," my mother would have said. "If I've learned anything, it's that Storytellers are rarely welcome anywhere." She would have said it, but we weren't speaking.

I am not like you. I may have dark skin and golden eyes, but I'm not an Ishva. I'm not a heretic. Those thoughts drove me to keep my head down, keep working hard. I was often the first intern to arrive at the Board of Public Information building each morning and the last to leave each night. I processed each report my superior set in front of me with diligent efficiency. When Ciereth Ashtar praised my work ethic, I thought I had never been so proud.

They caught the old man who was making the Ekati. A concerned citizen spotted him placing one of the glowing orbs on the edge of a fountain near my Upper School. He immediately confessed to smuggling the crystals from Ilthasia, but he insisted that he was no Storyteller. No matter how the Inquisitorial Guards questioned him (something I don't like to think about), he refused to give up his accomplice. The Storyteller could have run then, but she didn't.

Revolution was in the air. Sparks were starting to fly. In Pamalon's poorer quarters, people gathered in tight knots on street corners and whispered that it was high time for change, time for their voices to be heard. The street police ordered them to break up and move along. Most of them did so with nothing but a sullen glare, but a few fought back, and others cheered them on. It was as I had always feared. The spread of stories, the telling of too much truth, was on the verge of causing anarchy.

985, fifth year in the Council of Enlightened Unity

On a patch of blighted land near Pamalon's eastern gate, there's an old, crooked ewe tree. A single crystal sphere is buried beneath that tree, its soft blue light not bright enough to penetrate the foot of earth above it. Though I never used my mother's Storyteller magic before, it came naturally to me when I needed it most. As I told my story, images appeared in the air in front of me. The Ekati grew warm in my hands as it preserved my voice for all time. Maybe someone will dig it up in a hundred years. Or maybe someone will dig it up tomorrow, and it will mean my death.

I may have buried my story, but I can't bury my guilt. You see, I betrayed my own mother to the Board of Public Information. I don't remember deciding to do it. I didn't wake up one morning and think, this is the day I will turn my mother in for treason and sedition. What I do remember is being tired of the constant fear, the persistent sense that I am not enough for the country I have chosen to call my own. I remember asking Ciereth Ashtar for a private word at the end of an otherwise nondescript workday.

"I know who she is," I blurted out. My superior raised a skeptical eyebrow. "The Storyteller who's been stirring people up," I elaborated. "Her name . . . her name is Rayha Igonwe."

Once I said it, I couldn't unsay it. Nothing I said or did could call the Inquisitorial Guards back. I could have warned my mother, maybe, but then I would have just been tortured and put to death beside her.

Before that day, I didn't know a girl could feel almost insurmountable relief and guilt at the same time—relief that I had been a loyal patriot of Pamalon, guilt that it had cost me what I suspected was the best part of myself.

I have been able to leave the drugs behind after burying my Ekati. I still take long walks at night, prowling the foreign quarter like a ghost from one of Mother's old stories. Sometimes I look at my reflection in a mirror or a puddle and am convinced that I'm barely there, that I can see through my own skin. It's almost as if I'm already dead. Sometimes, on those long nocturnal walks, I look up at the tall stone buildings, wondering what it would be like to fling myself off the roof of one of them. Flying would be wonderful, even if it would only last for a few exhilarating heartbeats. Maybe I won't even feel the crash. But then I would have to face my dead mother and her dead sister Aekia and all of the slaughtered Ishva. Maybe they would all ask me, "How could you betray your own people, your own truth? Why did you do it?" But what I dread most, what wakes me up in a cold sweat, is the thought that the Ishva dead will understand me, that they will turn away and confirm my fear that no matter what I do, I will never belong in either land, in either world.

Sophie Trist is a Louisiana native and blind from birth. She's passionate about writing historical fiction and fantasy which explores marginalized communities and perspectives. Sophie is currently a second-year fiction candidate in the University of Arkansas's MFA program in creative writing. Her work appears in *Voyage YA Journal*, *Life Matters Journal*, *Spread Second Stories*, *The Braille Monitor*, and now *WINNERS*. When not reading or writing, Sophie can be found listening to country music or looking for a dog to play with.

THE IRONY OF EVERYTHING

Leah Reise

The asteroid was only hours away. Everything would disappear in the blink of an eye. And yet, the moon shone so beautifully, like it would exist until the end of time.

No surprise there. It was always brilliant and bright despite our minuscule lives, our self-proclaimed grandeur, our pollution, and our politics. It had always shone in spite of us.

None of the villagers stayed indoors tonight. What was the point? There would be no village. There would be no people. Soon, there would be no planet—as if it had never even existed, because without people and memories, no one would pass on its story—an entire planet lost in the empty wind of space.

So I would swing from this tree until the time came—on the tree that had existed before our people built our village here—from the same rope and wooden seat that our great-grandparents had carved and hung from this branch that still held strong. It was ironic, really, that, like the moon, the tree seemed perpetual when in a matter of hours the moon that had circled the Earth for four billion years would be nothing but particles amongst the stars, and this very tree that had stood sturdy for over a century would not even be ash.

Why then as I swung until my death with the wind against my face was I laughing uncontrollably? Perhaps it was because I'd come to realize moments ago that having lived at all during this fantastical blink of time was something of an ironic wonder. To have lived at all when nothing should have lived or even existed to begin with was a spectacular phenomenon in itself. Life alone was its own anomaly.

As I faced the cosmos that would soon consume me, I wondered if any part of my consciousness would go on. I didn't believe in deities or magic, but since my youth I felt part of a circle of life, a quantum existence of sorts, an interconnected series of events that ultimately resulted in me—all my cells and neurological pathways, every tiny atom that would soon return to the source of absolutely everything and nothing all at once. Not only me, of course. I was but a tiny piece in the story of the cosmos—just like everyone else, just like whatever else existed clear across the opposite end of the universe.

As I swung and laughed and cursed the vast abyss above, I also came to reckon with its amazing elements and with its beauty. Every tiny human consciousness on this tiny planet in this tiny blink of time at least had the chance *to be*. To love. To laugh. To have. To feel. To experience this blue marble through the eyes of a multifaceted complex and emotional race.

Did the universe experience it with us? I wondered. Were we but vessels in some grand experiment? Or, were we but a tiny mutation in a chaotic course of random events of cause and effect that just so happened to allow the universe to experience itself through us? Did the universe experience its own ironic existence through all creatures on Earth down to every tiny multicellular organism? Or was everything interwoven for no other reason but to exist?

My mind spun into a sticky mess as the wind blew through my hair and the asteroid crept closer. In the not-so-far-off distance of space, our doom was quite the beauty. The brightest ball of fire in the sky. Another irony. How could the thing that would destroy us all look so damn beautiful amidst the vibrant solar system?

Classical music commenced from behind me, encapsulating the fleeting night with a fluid departure of melancholy elegance. We would all go out with great splendor, it seemed. We wouldn't leave this world, this plane of existence, with anything but style. So be it.

"John," my father called to me light-heartedly but with bated breath from the bonfire below the hill. "Come join us. Drink with us."

I'd already made my peace with him. I'd told him I loved him for the first time in I wasn't sure how many years. Since that raw moment between us, I felt like a child again. It had taken the end of the world to open me up, and here we were, father and son, dying together. Two lonely men putting to rest their differences and facing the flames vulnerable and exposed. Why not? I wouldn't have it any other way.

I pivoted on the swing to face him. "I'm content here," I called back. His uneasy green eyes held a whole world of sorrows in them, but he smiled solemnly, and I smiled back.

They'd told us our deaths would be quick, so we weren't afraid. In the moment the 20-mile-wide rock hit our atmosphere, the explosion would kill us in seconds. The sight would likely be breathtaking . . . and yes, I meant that quite literally, pun and all.

I hadn't heard any cries tonight, not even from the children. They had no idea what was to come. On the contrary, tonight was most exciting for them. Their laughter and dancing around the fire set my heart soaring free into the warm breeze and brilliant night sky. My eyes set on our incoming death-mail from outer space with awe. The giant ball of light grew bigger every minute, for it was like its own sun. Tears streamed down my face at its beauty. So much for not crying tonight, but it was truly the most amazing sight I'd ever see. I had always been quite the star gazer, and this was without a doubt the motherlode of them all.

"John." A soft feminine voice impaled my chest like a swift blade to the heart.

For the slightest moment, I just stared at the moon, seemingly lost within its craters. That voice . . . I let my head turn toward its source. "Sage . . ." Her name leaving my lips almost felt surreal. "What are you doing here?"

"I came to find you. My family is there by the fire." A tear beaded down her cheek as her head motioned toward her humble parents who embraced on a log, her parents who were always kind to me. "We figured tonight was a good night to come back here. There are so many memories in this place." Her words were frail and embodied with pain, but she looked at me fondly with the purest colors of emotion in her eyes.

Seeing that very emotion, which I realized she'd held onto all these years, tore the hole that now lived under my sternum wider than it already was—the vulnerable place inside me that had given way earlier tonight when I'd forgiven my father. It only took a moment's gaze into her large caramel eyes to lose myself to the past. In that moment, I was no longer ready to die. She had been my everything once. She had left me. And she was back *now*?! Now that nothing was left to behold? I felt a rage that I knew was only my deeply suppressed love for her boil to the surface. Because I didn't want to end this night—this end to everything—with anything sour, I turned toward the moon and hoped its innocent and stunning shine would draw the gurgling burn beneath my chest into the atmosphere. Draw it away from me. I pleaded with the moon.

That's when she laid her warm hand upon my shoulder, and without warning a horrid cry left my chest. I was embarrassed. I was terrified. I was so many things I hadn't been only minutes ago. Just like she used to do, she had strung a rope of fire around my heart and tied a knot so tight that I could barely breathe. Sage threw her arms around my neck and collapsed on top of me with sobs that mirrored my own. The silky ebony skin of her arms shimmered in the moonlight like she was an ethereal creature from another world. Somewhere warm and delightful. Somewhere that wasn't going to disappear into nothing in a matter of minutes.

"I'm so sorry," I cried. "I'm so sorry for everything I've . . ."

"John, please don't apologize. It wasn't your fault. I never blamed you. We were young. We weren't ready. I knew you loved me. I always knew. That's why I'm here. To tell you that I never stopped loving you. Not once. Not ever."

Hearing her say those words brought so many conflicting emotions. It was like my chest had imploded and then turned inside out, spilling out into a wave that could engulf the world. That's what she had always done to me.

Before anything more could be said or done, the light in the sky grew brighter, appearing like a sun next to the moon.

"Is there room for two on that old swing?" she said sweetly.

I gazed at her one last time and opened my arms. She sat carefully atop my lap and I wrapped my arms snuggly around her, in such a way that nothing could ever separate us, not even death. Our gazes turned up to the stars and the moon and the night sky we would never see again. A sort of peacefulness enveloped me and in that moment I knew it had filled her too, because she leaned ever so delicately against my chest and breathed in deeply as the fiery ball engulfed the sky.

Leah Reise is a frontline health-care professional, novelist, and writer who has a Bachelor's Degree in Spanish from Sonoma State University. She also completed additional undergraduate studies in anthropology at San Francisco State University, and social and biological sciences have greatly influenced her life and writing. Her first article, "Open Letter to the People of Sonoma County," about social justice was published in the Sonoma County *Peace Press* in August of 2000. Her first novel series, *The Beauty in Darkness,* is a trilogy: *A Vampire Story* was published in 2016, *A New Race* was published in 2020, and the sequel is a work in progress. "The Irony of Everything," one of her latest short stories, was the Grand Prize Winner in the Dystopian category of SOOP's 1st Annual Short Story contest in 2021.

LIANA AND THE SEVENTH SPIN

Roberta Azzopardi

She had always known that house on the small crest by the sea—the one the sea teases playfully, waves lapping at the very foot of the stairs that led to its blue door. A natural stone breakwater jutted over the water a few hundred metres away, enclosing the small cove like a one-armed embrace. The house gazed placidly, four windows for four eyes and a small wrought-iron balcony that sat like a frown between them. Vines had crept up one of its walls, leaves brushing each other, lifting and falling with the currents of the wind, a clingy lover that fawned in worship. It seemed to her a stoic dwelling, cynical, arrogant almost, in the way it stood erect. It existed outside of everything, outside of space, outside of time. Permanent, out of place, odd. A bit like her.

"That place is cursed. Don't go near." Her mother would frown, wrap the shawl tighter about her and give the house a fleetingly ugly look—as if she were afraid of resting her eyes on it for too long.

"Don't go near, I'm warning you." Her father pointed an accusing finger at her, like she had already done what he was warning her against. She looked away as he sighed, wiped his sweaty forehead with the dirt-streaked sleeve, stopping to lean on the rake he held. She crouched and dropped a few seeds in the trench he had dug out, watched as he rolled the soil over them, burying them. Around her, father, son, mother and daughter repeated the same act over and over, season after season, until the young were young no more and crossed the trench to take the rake, until death claimed them too.

Sometimes, it felt to her that death had already claimed her.

She existed with the seasons and unlike the house, she existed inside them too, with the planting and the harvest, with fine lines becoming deeper on her mother's face and hair growing whiter on her father's head. Nothing else changed. Nothing else happened. It was stifling.

Don't go near. Don't go near. Don't go near. The house held her only fascination. It too never changed, even when it should. Even when no one tended the garden, or painted the door, or maintained the roof, that should have holes sometimes like everyone else's. Even when no one went in or came out, when no light came on at night, the house never changed—like a fly in an amber stone. And it was perhaps this atemporality, this existence beyond anything that was natural, that scared the superstitious village. When a group of curious boys once got close enough to peek inside a back window, they claimed an ivy branch had wrapped itself around their ankles in warning. They ran, leaving the house in peace.

Whenever the sun or the moon hit that small window at the top, and the house looked like a cyclops, she bit down on the urge to stand up, walk down the path that led to the cove, climb up the tendrils she knew would never hurt her, and peer inside. Instead, she would go to her bed, face the other way, curl up and let sleep carry her off.

··◆◆◆◆◆··

She never remembered her dreams, except that one time she felt, rather than remembered, that she had fallen from tremendous heights, waking up suddenly, her heart racing. She sat up, auburn hair tumbling over her shoulders. Her eyes were wide in her reflection, like they had seen something she was desperately trying to recall but couldn't. The memory slipped from her fingers like silk thread. Gradually her heartbeat slowed, returning to the dull throb she was more accustomed to. What adventure had she been on at night?

"Liana! I made your favourite breakfast! Don't let it get cold!"

It was Liana's eighteenth birthday, no longer a child, though the thought did not excite her. Already the boys had started looking at her differently, having apparently forgotten little, odd Liana. Liana avoided their gazes, afraid they would interpret her glance as interest where there was none. No one shared her curiosity, her desire to truly live, in the way she would sometimes run down a hill so she could feel her heart pounding in her chest like it wanted to burst free—just to prove to herself that she was alive. It was no one's fault. She had always been the strange one. With age, something else had started to happen, alongside the curves she had unwillingly developed—a continual dull ache at the base of her back, perhaps emanating from the mounting desperation at what she imagined the rest of her life to look like. When her bleeding appeared for the first time with the full moon, she remembered her mother's glow. *You can marry and have children in a few years*, she had whispered . . . as if fulfilling Liana's secret desire. Liana had not understood then what it meant. She was still a child for all intents and purposes. It was different now and that ache did not arrive only with the full moon anymore. It was present continuously—a tangible dread at what life here had in store for her.

"Li-ANA!"

"I'm coming." She jumped out of bed, wriggled out of her cotton night dress and into her blue one, a faded coarse thing with a white hem at the bottom. The smell of eggs and pancakes rose to meet her as she descended the stairs. A quick peck on the cheek from mother and father, coffee brought to the table as opposed to her customary brewing responsibility, and a plate with thin slices of pancakes loaded with syrup—the only variations in an otherwise normal day. As she licked her spoon clean, eyes closed, her father opened the door.

"Let's go."

$$\cdot\cdot\blacklozenge\ \blacklozenge\ \blacklozenge\ \blacklozenge\cdot\cdot$$

The sun was relentless. Liana shielded her gaze and squinted. Already her dress stuck to her back with sweat, her fingers grimy.

She looked down.

At her feet, just as she was about to step over it, something shiny caught her eye. She scooped it up and held it in front of her eyes, between her thumb and index finger. It was round and cold to the touch, like it had not had time to absorb the heat yet. It was a metal of some sort, though it had a pearly finish she had never seen anywhere else. On one side, it was smooth and slightly rounded while on the other, a serrated hole pierced it. Liana frowned as she turned it around in her hand and tried to guess its use. The hole seemed to have been designed to fit around something—like a knob.

"Liana! Why are you stopping?" Liana put her small treasure inside her pocket and moved on dropping seeds, her mind distracted.

·· ◆ ◆ ◆ ◆ ◆ ·

Later, she'd say she had been called to her window where she now sat, her hair framing her soft face, the object lying cold in the palm of her hand—called there to see a blinding white light flickering twice from the topmost window in the attic on the house by the sea. She recalled the shock, the way her mouth formed a perfect O of surprise, like the suddenness of the moment needed a way out.

But just as quickly, it was gone, like lightning on a clear day. Liana stood up, backed away a couple of steps. The pearly knob throbbed in her closed palm like it had acquired a life of its own and it matched, beat by beat, her own racing heart. She grabbed her cloak, threw it over her white cotton nightdress and silently made her way out. She paused in front of the path that led to the house. How often had she lingered here, toeing the dirt trail she never dared to take? Had she been afraid of her parents, the villagers? Or was she scared she would be disappointed? That the house would turn out to be nothing but an abandoned dwelling that time was kind to? All her hopes of something happening in her life had been pinned on this house . . . if it turned out to be nothing, then her very life, she felt, would turn out to be the same.

Liana tucked her hair behind her ear twice and stepped forward.

· · ✦ ✦ ◆ ✦ ✦ · ·

The house felt larger than it looked, the vines both soft and strong beneath her touch as she started making her way up the wall. They were a few layers deep, providing a secure foothold. She turned her face against the crisp wind so it could brush her hair away from the front of her eyes, until she was finally there, at the edge of the crescent window. She breathed deeply, stepped up and peered in.

The room was largely empty, the wooden ceiling slanted like the roof outside. The floor was littered with scraps of paper, and a tall, gilded mirror leaned against the beams directly opposite the window. A table formed an angle against the roof, empty but for some loose paper and a strange circular object that spilled its metal contents for the woman who sat in front of it. Liana's eyes widened as she held the vines tighter, her knuckles turning white. The woman's back was straight, her hair gathered in a soft chignon at the nape of her long neck. She wore a loose dress with a wide neckline and flowing sleeves secured just below her chest with a thin rope-like belt. The colour was like nothing Liana had ever seen anyone wearing in Soverleen, a deep ruby red like the setting sun, with wide pleats at the bottom. She was writing on the papers, stopping occasionally to fiddle with the object in front of her. There was something familiar in her fluid movements, in the way she held her arm as she wrote. Without looking, Liana knew the writing would be slanted like the ceiling overhead, though she did not know how she knew. She waited with bated breath, following the woman's gestures until the moment she stood up and, still with her back to Liana, walked to the mirror. With one last look at the papers and the object she left on the table, she stepped into the mirror, whose substance rippled like water, swallowing her whole in a blinding flash. Then, like a curtain at the village's small theatre, the entire room went dark and Liana felt her feet slipping, like the vines couldn't be bothered to provide a hold anymore. She hastened to get down, nearly falling as the branches went limp and soft. She jumped, breathing hard, her hands against the wall, eyes to the ground.

What she had just witnessed went beyond reason, and yet, she never, for one second, doubted what she had seen. Hesitantly, she walked around the house—that stood indifferently as it always had— and tried the front door. Locked. When she went to stand in front of the window again at the back of the house, the moon had turned it white, like the pearly surface of the knob that was still in her pocket. She gazed hard, her heart dancing in her chest with the same thrill and uncontained happiness that the first explorers of an unknown land must have felt.

· · ◆ ◆ ◆ ◆ · ·

And so it was that for the next few days, as the same white light flashed twice from the window heralding the woman's arrival, Liana ran to watch a similar scene unfold before her. That it was the same woman every time was not immediately clear. On the second day, a woman dressed in a long white dress, a gold belt secured below her chest and a thick necklace of a blue stone Liana had never seen before, sat at the desk, shuffling through papers, writing some notes of her own, assembling and disassembling the mystery object before her. At first, with her golden skin tone and straight jet-black hair brushing her shoulders, Liana was sure it could not be the same woman with the soft chignon, until in a gesture that looked more like despair, the woman leaned against her chair and pulled at her hair, revealing the same—though much shorter—soft, curling, dark auburn hair from the day before. A wig! She placed the deceiving item on the table and, arms glittering with gold bracelets, she set about adjusting the small items before her, consulting her papers, taking something out and placing another back inside. The items, too small to make out, somehow seemed to fit inside the larger circular object. But when the woman got up with the same slow movements Liana felt like she knew intimately, the object still had its entrails spilled about it. She picked up the wig, placed it back on her head and, after one long sigh, she walked to the mirror, feet slapping against the hard stone in her golden sandals, and disappeared again. This time, Liana was already sliding back down with more ease. The door and every other window in the house, however, were still locked, a secret now forthcoming, now barring.

Knowing there was a pattern to the madness, Liana anticipated the next arrival and, although it was doubly hard to get to the high window with vines that turned unforgivingly dewy and slippery, she made it on the third day just in time to see the woman step out of the mirror. Liana peered carefully, catching a glimpse of the face, slightly rounded at the cheekbones and getting sharper at the chin in a heart shape, but the woman's movements were too quick for her to distinguish facial features. She was wearing a long skirt made of animal hide and a small band that wound around her breasts and covered little else. Her hair was long and straight, a dark brown that caught the moon's light as it swayed with her movements to sit down. In one hand, she held a spear, but, from her other closed palm, out tumbled three shiny items which she placed next to the ones she herself had left behind the day before. She placed the spear gently against the table, pulled the papers towards her and started the now familiar process of reading, writing and assembling the item in front of her (for now Liana was sure that that was indeed what she was trying to do).

Every night continued the same. As the seasons rolled naturally, so did the woman step out of and back inside the mirror without fail.

She wore thick furry jackets and a hood that enlarged her head four times over, boots still flecked with snow, her face ruddy from the cold, and in her hand a small wheel with a thin needle-like item.

She wore a long, satin dress in bold colours and decorated with small pink flowers that wrapped around her tightly, forcing her to take small steps. Her face was deadly pale. In her hair, two sticks held a bun and in her hand five little balls made a tinkling sound as she lay them on the table.

She wore a beautiful velvet gown with a pearl netting in her hair and a small pouch around her waist from which she procured two crown-like instruments. She tucked a stray lock of hair behind her ear, twice.

She wore bonnets, hats, crowns and scarves, long dresses and short dresses with frills and tassels. She wore trousers like a man, aprons, gold and diamonds. She had clean hands and a dirty face. She had long hair and short hair but always the same colour. And always, always, she was bearing items.

Liana watched, her heart in her throat as the item on the table grew smaller and then bigger, smaller and bigger again until the contents all but vanished, each lodged meticulously inside. Every day she wondered at the woman—at who she was, at what she was doing, where she was going. Something stirred inside her when she once had a clearer look at her face. It troubled her, the way she felt she knew her face and yet had never seen her before. The determination with which she stepped in and out of fate. Liana longed to be her or, at least, to step inside that room to talk to her. But she did not dare tap against the window. Whatever the woman was doing seemed to be of extreme importance and Liana was afraid she would upset the equilibrium which seemed to hold everything perfectly balanced. Like the house that suffered nothing, she too did not wish to cause any trouble.

And yet . . .

And yet, that little pearly knob she had found all those days ago, exactly on the first day of the woman's appearance, was that not tied to this event? Could it not also be part of the mysterious object the woman was building? Surely, if that were the case, the house would let her in? And yet, even the vines made it clear she was not welcome once the woman disappeared. She was unwanted . . . at least, Liana thought as she made her slow way back home one night, at least for now.

· · ✦ ✦ ◆ ✦ ✦ · ·

But she had not been the only one to witness the strange light flashing every night from the little window shaped like a moon.

At first, little Sally believed it to be the moon and thought nothing of it. But when it was repeated two, three, four times, she started fearing monsters lurking beneath her bed, brought forth from the terrible house by the sea. When she told her mother, it took the sensible lady a couple more days to stay up at night and see for herself what her daughter was harping about every single morning. What she saw terrified her. Very soon, the entire village knew of the strange happenings and, much to Liana's dismay, the elders decided that 'something must be done'. Though what that something was remained uncertain.

"Surely it's just a prank from one of Garrett's boys," Liana said one day, as she wiped the dishes with her mother. Her father was smoking his pipe, gazing intently into the fire like he could see something no one else could. Her mother shivered.

"I always knew something was wrong with that house. We should have burned it down long ago."

"Burn it?" Liana stopped, hand hovering over the little china plate with a chink at the top. It was her father who answered with a grunt.

"They're thinking of burning it down with the full moon. The priest said it would be auspicious."

"But that's . . . that's tonight." Liana hadn't realised she had gripped the plate, the one with the chink at the top and little flowers forming a garland around the edge. When it shattered on the tiles at her feet, the flowers scattered, the chain broken.

"Oh look what you've done, Liana!" Her mother bent forward to collect the larger pieces. But Liana was still staring at her father, who turned on his seat, craning his neck to look at his daughter.

"So it is," he said, taking a puff from his pipe as he surveyed the scene, his eyes finally resting on her. "You'll stay put, let the men handle this." And he shifted his gaze away, like that settled matters.

That day, the first flashes of light came earlier, when the sun had not yet set, like it knew something had gone very wrong. Liana left through her bedroom window and ran, hoping no one had seen the flashes so early in the day. But when she had climbed the tendrils, each leaf pushing against the soles of her feet, and peered inside the room, there was no one there. Liana stared at the still mirror, at the object on the table that now looked complete though she still could not figure out what it was, at the papers waiting for the woman to rifle them through. But no woman came, even though the room remained as clear as day and the vines sturdy and secure. Liana climbed back down and rushed to the front door just as the sun completely set and dusk stretched its dark fingers across the sky. Already the moon hung pale and full, a patient marker, an omen of the end.

Liana stood in front of the door and tucked her hair twice behind her ear. Her heart had lodged itself somewhere, making an awful racket against her ribcage in the dead silence. The door was ajar.

The lapping sound of the waves disappeared the moment she stepped inside, like she had travelled somewhere far with just one stride. The house was empty but clean, no coat of dust covered the floors, the mantelpiece, the wooden balustrade. Dark outlines where portraits once hung. The silence was absolute, the air smelled of wax and honey somehow, lavender, strange spices, sandalwood. She followed the strange scents that mingled and took her far away, to places she had never been but somehow still knew. Patchouli and musk. With every step, her gait grew more confident. Jasmine and rosewater. She had been here before, many times.

She climbed the stairs to reach the attic and paused inside the room. There stood the mirror, there the moon shaped window and there the table with paper and . . . the object.

She walked towards it first and leaned forward so she could look at it at eye level. It was as big as the span of her hand and four fingers thick. On one side, it had the face of an unfamiliar clock. There were no numbers, but strange symbols, a completely different alphabet. Instead of hands, the sun, the moon and other bodies which could sometimes be observed in the night sky were scattered across its face, still and dull. At the top of the strange clock, an abrupt and jagged nail with a flat head pierced the implement and stood out like a button waiting to be pressed. Liana touched it but it was too hard to bend or be pushed back. The back was plain and unadorned, a little dent at the top marked the spot where it could be opened.

She turned now to the papers scattered on the table. Slowly, like a sacred ritual she was initiating, she sat down and started reading.

Rome, AD1497. First spin.

The two items were retrieved from the tomb of Saint Peter in a little hole in the wall indicated by the Seeker. Beware of the Borgia Pope. He has seen you and has taken a liking to you. He must in no way get close to you.

I have taken the first of the crowns and placed it right beneath Mercury, where it lodged on its own, seemingly attracted like a magnet. The second I placed directly above, at an angle, like so.

Next to the words, a little diagram of the inside of the clock was drawn, with arrows and instructions. Liana blinked, grabbed another page, unsure what it was she had just read, hoping that the more she read, the more the picture would come together.

Kyoto, AD1600. Third Spin.

The orbs were still located at Fushimi-Inari Taisha, but moved marginally due to the Earth's differently tilted axis. The trip was, thankfully, uneventful but remember, if you see the

horse bolt, you must stop it, or it will kill Date Masamune. The
Guide has told you of the samurai's importance in years to come.

The five orbs I have placed descending, not ascending in size
this time, starting from Mercury, and ending with Jupiter.

Liana shook her head. With shaking fingers she turned the pages over scanning the familiar swirls in the words, breathing in the scent of ink and old papers. Tulum, AD1132. Fourth Spin. Persepolis, BC500. Second Spin. Kansas, AD1962. Sixth Spin. Pompei, BC50. First Spin. And again. Tulum, Rome, Persepolis, Granada, Nairobi, Melbourne, Sao Paolo. First Spin, Second, Third up until the Sixth. Her eyes grew wider with each affirmation, with each variation in instructions, with each dated adventure that seemed to be repeated and only slightly different every time. Six times she visited every location on the same year, points that spanned the entire globe, places Liana had never heard about in the limited schooling she had received, places that did not exist yet. Six times she had retrieved the same items and attempted to build this . . . this celestial clock.

With her fingers she trailed the name at the end of every entry, a signature of sorts. With it, memories she never knew she had stored, were freed.

Elena. אֱלִיעֶנָה. Helen. Liane. Ηλιάνα. Elienah. اناييلا. Illeana. *Liana.*

Whispers in her head, from people who had long gone or who were still to come. All the names she had been called by across time and space. Relief flooded her as the caged feeling she had suffered her whole life lifted, the sweetest moment of her entire life. *Finally.*

Outside, someone shouted and a rock was thrown, breaking the glass in the moon window. Liana turned, narrowed her eyes. It was time. She stood up, took the little pearly knob from her pocket and hesitated. Downstairs, the fire had already started raging, swallowing the house. Her hand hovered over the Course Corrector, feeling its energy radiating. Would this time be the one? Will she carry it to the safety of the White Haven? She chewed the inside of her mouth, but the smoke had already started slipping through the crack under the door. So she held the powerful instrument in her arm like a precious bundle, pushed the knob down and turned it sharply anticlockwise. The world bended on itself and merged in one straight hole through which she fell and fell and fell.

···✦ ✦✦ ✦✦··

Liana opened her eyes, hugged herself and cursed.

"Damn it."

"Indeed. Seventh time lucky?" She accepted the hand that was offered her and got up, brushing her skirt and tucking her hair behind her ear. Twice. The Guide was looking at her with a lopsided grin, his face as timeless as himself.

"That's what you said the third time."

"And the fourth, fifth, sixth." They started walking away from the little circular pad she had landed on, down a white path and between white walls. Above them, the roof was open to a limpid blue sky. Two large moons hung above them, one white, one blue.

"What was it this time, do you know?" Liana asked stretching her neck this way and that. The Guide shook his head. He was not much taller than her, but it always felt like he was. A towering, warm presence.

"It could be any slight variation in the gears or oscillator. You need to figure it out Eleyna." She groaned softly, pinching the bridge of her nose.

"I'm starting to think there's a missing piece." The Guide looked at her, though not in surprise.

"What makes you think that?" Eleyna gestured with her hands, feeling the ghost of the Course Corrector in her arms. She shrugged.

"I've started feeling when a piece is in its proper place. The Corrector sucks it in and it vibrates, just a little." She shook her head. "I was sure I had it this time." The Guide smiled at her.

"Then perhaps you need to find that missing piece by yourself."

"But it could be anywhere, any century . . . how can I find it if even the Seeker wasn't able to?" They had arrived at a little patch of garden on top of a gently sloping hill. A familiar olive tree, its trunk thick and old and carved by millennia, stood at the top, the same olive tree from which the dove broke off a branch to give to Noah after the flood. The Guide had stopped, placed a reverential hand on the bark.

"You're not looking hard enough where it matters." He said slowly. Eleyna bit her lip.

"I don't understand."

"Why are you so quick to dismiss the one that brought you here?"

"Liana?" Eleyna's eyes went wide, as the Guide smiled.

"Your true self, the one who braved the house against all odds. The one who yearned for bigger things, the one who had dreams, who paved the way for you. Here." He paused, cocking his head to one side. "Or have you forgotten?"

She hadn't. Shame rose to her cheeks as she realized how Liana had taken on the weakest shade in her colourful lives, how her life started mattering less and less, even when she knew she owed all her lives to her.

"I thought there could only be that one last piece. But you're right."

He grinned, "I am always right. Helps to know everything and be everywhere at once I suppose, but still. It takes work."

"Sure." But she too grinned in return, squaring her shoulders and turning to face him. "I'm ready."

"You know the rules."

Eleyna rolled her eyes. "Don't alter the course of history. Changing the fabric of time is why the Course Corrector is needed in the first place," she said in a sing-song voice. She coughed at the look from the Guide. "Time is relative," she continued soberly. "Liana will experience day-to-day changes but in the mirror's parallel worlds, time is infinite."

"Good. And?"

"Only Liana's memories are erased every time she—and I—wake up on her eighteenth birthday."

"Thus closing the loop. Good." He looked at her, his face softening. "Godspeed." He leaned forward and touched her forehead.

When she opened her eyes, she found herself in a lavender meadow. Provence, AD1254. Hélène sighed and closed her eyes again. He had been right. Time had found Liana for a reason and she needed to enter that shade of her life with more faith in her true self. Liana might have no memories, but ideas can linger much, much longer and she needed to implant the right kind in herself first. The kind that whispered—*I believe in you.*

She stood up between rows of swaying lavender.

"Le septième, c'est la bonne."

The Seventh Spin had begun.

Roberta Azzopardi's love for literature and the written word goes back to her childhood, penning mystery stories after consuming the one-too-many Nancy Drew novella. Throughout the years, this calling never abandoned her, as she sought to refine her writing through formal writing courses and assignments, as well as dabbling in different mediums to express herself. Her blog, words.com.mt, was set up to reach a wider audience through her writing of short stories, opinion pieces, and reflections. Liana and The Seventh Spin is her first story to be published in an anthology, and she is in the process of editing the second draft of a novel set in Florence in the fifteenth century. Roberta lives in Malta with her husband and son.

GREETINGS FROM EARTH

Preston Dennett

M y beautiful wife and I inched forward in line. "So crowded," she said, holding my arm as somebody jostled against her. "We shouldn't have come."

I knew how she hated crowds. But we were in the area and who could pass up the opportunity to view an actual alien artifact?

I had visited it before, of course, but Michelle never had. And she always had some reason to avoid seeing it. We lived so close; she could see it anytime, she would say. Or, I've seen pictures of it on TV. How different could it be in real life?

But I insisted. She was an artist, and I just instinctively knew that there was something about this artifact that she had to see.

I was right. Michelle peered ahead of us in line. The artifact was just barely visible hidden by trees in a field up ahead. Already, she was clearly impressed.

"Oh," she said. "I see it. It's beautiful."

"I told you," I said. "I knew you'd like it."

She gripped my arm more tightly as we moved ahead in line and the artifact came into unobstructed view.

I loved the fact that this thing from another world continued to mystify the scientists. It had appeared overnight in a little field outside of Stockton, California. A perfect sphere, just shy of 130 meters in diameter, sunk slightly into the ground. At first glance, it appeared to be made of emerald. It was shiny, reflective, almost translucent. Closer, it looked like ceramic, or even stone or metal. But it wasn't. Nor was it plastic or glass. Nobody knew what the heck it was.

From what I had read about it, the artifact was absolutely impervious to everything we had thrown at it. It didn't react to chemical or acid tests, diamond drills, explosives, or X-rays. What it came down to, nobody had any idea what it was.

Naturally speculation ran wild as to its purpose. Some said it was a crashed spaceship and when we finally opened it, we would find the alien bodies. Others speculated that it was a probe, sent to monitor our planet. There were dozens of theories: an alien library, an alien bomb, a piece of alien art. The only thing people could agree upon: it was definitely not from Earth.

It took years, and more than a few lawsuits, before the artifact finally became open to the public. Now, it was nothing more than a tourist attraction.

Perhaps, I thought, *that* was its purpose.

By the time it was our turn to approach, Michelle was digging her nails painfully into my arm. Her entire body trembled.

"Are you okay?" I asked. This was classic Michelle. Sensitive, emotional, dramatic.

"It's just so beautiful," she said breathlessly. I could see she was beginning to cry. The sphere towered above us, and Michelle seemed both afraid and in awe, while at the same time attracted to it.

"Are you sure you're all right?" I asked again. She ignored me and was now totally mesmerized by the object.

Around us, the other tourists laughed. They oohed and ahhed. They posed in front of the artifact and took pictures. They talked about where they would visit next.

Michelle, however, appeared to be struggling to breathe. She looked like she was about to faint when suddenly she let go of my arm and stumbled toward the object. She stood next to it and placed her hands softly against its surface.

I smiled. Michelle had always been sensitive to what she called "energies" and I had seen her do this type of thing before. She often shocked people by blurting out psychic snippets of their lives, or telling them that she sensed a spirit in their house. It freaked some people out, but it was one of many things I have always loved about my wife. She's different from anyone else I've ever met. And with those olive-green eyes and auburn hair, well . . . for me it was love at first sight. For her, it took a little convincing.

Michelle looked over at me, an alarmed expression on her face. I saw tears forming in her eyes. I was about to jump forward when it happened. The sphere swallowed her.

It happened so fast. All at once there was a loud humming noise, the sphere lit up bright green, and there was a blinding flash.

The crowd screamed and I watched my wife tumble inside the sphere.

The glow faded away.

I stared numbly at the artifact, disbelieving. Where was my wife? Had it actually taken my wife?

The artifact now appeared normal—except the crowd of tourists was screaming and running around in pandemonium. And Michelle was gone.

I leapt forward and beat my fists against it, screaming. Nothing. I stood back, my head spinning. My wife was inside that thing.

Guards converged and began to usher the crowd away from the artifact. A particularly strong-looking guard approached me. I whirled to face him and set myself ready to fight. Seeing my stance, he held out his stunner. I stood my ground.

"I'm not leaving," I said. "That thing just ate my wife."

The guard's expression changed from anger to shock and he lowered his stunner. He approached and grabbed my arm. "Come with me. People are going to want to talk to you."

I shook off his arm and choked back my tears. "Then bring them here. I'm not going anywhere."

The guard paused, looked around, and nodded. "Don't go anywhere," he said.

I laughed dryly. "Right."

He nodded again and left me alone and ordered another guard to stay with me.

The remaining tourists were quickly cleared away, and I stood there in the shadow of the evil and ugly thing that had kidnapped my wife. How could I have done this to her? This was completely my fault. I shouldn't have made her come. I knew how sensitive she was. I should have known that something like this would happen. Michelle always had a way of cutting straight through all the crap right to the truth of things. But I never could have imagined that she would do this to the artifact. Or that it would take her!

I stared up at it, still in a state of shock. I wondered if, even now, Michelle could see me, down on my knees, weeping, calling her name, and shouting obscenities at the object, demanding that it give back my wife.

The artifact remained silent as stone.

Shortly later, officials began to arrive, first one, then another, and soon many. I told each of them what had happened. Each of them in turn asked me about Michelle. Was I sure she had gone inside this thing? What was so special about her? Why her?

What could I tell them? Michelle *was* special. She *was* different from most people. She was a little bit psychic, I told them. I don't know if they believed me, but Michelle had convinced me of her powers long ago. I no longer had the luxury of disbelief.

The questions continued. Soon, even more highly placed officials arrived and wanted me to answer all the questions again.

"Now listen!" I shouted angrily. "If you think . . ."

At that moment, the sphere emitted a loud humming noise and began to brighten. Its brightness increased and there was a bright flash, and it was gone. I thought I caught an after-image of it darting upwards, but I couldn't be sure.

It had taken my wife!

No! It hadn't. There was Michelle, standing where the object had been, looking up. Tears poured from her eyes. She was shaking.

All eyes focused on her. I watched her head dart back and forth as she searched the crowd for me. She saw me and we locked gazes. She smiled weakly and promptly fainted.

She was in my arms before she hit the ground. Chaos erupted around me. Three guards pounced on me and pulled me from my wife. Michelle was scooped up and taken out of my sight. I was pinned to the ground. I did my best to free myself and, as a result, I was roughly handcuffed. I screamed for my wife, but my pleas were ignored.

I didn't see Michelle for three days. She was placed in a military hospital where I was told she was recovering fine and was undergoing questioning. True to my nature, I raised a huge protest and demanded to see her. I was told calmly to be patient, that she would be released shortly, and that I should go home to wait by my phone. Of course, I refused to leave and had to be escorted home by armed guards.

I stewed in our apartment, watching the news while my wife was portrayed as everything from an alien traitor to a galactic iconoclast, someone who gets off on destroying alien artifacts.

Finally, I got the call. Michelle was ready to come home.

"You look like hell," I said, as I drove out of the parking lot. "Are you okay?" She looked a mess, but she also looked strangely content, almost amused.

"I'm fine," she said. "Just angry and tired. I haven't slept for three days. I'll tell you everything, but first I need to sleep, and eat, and shower. God, I must stink." She sank into her seat, reclined it and closed her eyes. In moments, she was asleep.

I carried her into our bedroom and tucked her in.

It was around sundown when I finally heard her creep into the bathroom and start the shower. I quickly fixed up some coffee and a snack of fresh-cut fruit and toast.

Michelle came out of the bedroom, newly scrubbed and wrapped in her thick blue cotton robe. She plopped herself down at the table and began sipping the coffee, black and strong and very hot, just how she liked it.

"You know, you're all over the news," I said. "You wouldn't believe what a fuss you've caused. Everybody wants to know who you are and what happened to you."

Michelle looked up at me with that secret mischievous smile that she knows makes me putty in her hands.

"What about you?" she asked. "Don't you want to know?"

I smiled. "More than anything."

"You're not going to believe it," she said. "Everybody was wrong about the artifact. None of the theories was right. Not even close. You should've seen the faces on the government suits when I told them what it actually was. They were not happy. They didn't believe me. It took me three days to convince them. I'm still not sure if they believe me."

"Okay, already! You are such a tease. What was it? Tell me."

"Fine, I'll tell you." Michelle's eyebrows popped up. "No, better yet. I'll show you. Be right back."

My wife hopped up from her chair and dashed up the staircase into the loft. I couldn't imagine what she was looking for. There was nothing up there but the stuff we almost never used but just couldn't throw away. Christmas ornaments? Was that what the artifact was? What else did we have stored up there? Old winter clothes, some old furniture, photographs, trophies from school.

Michelle danced into the room carrying a small book.

"Have you seen one of these before?"

She slid the book across the table and began munching on her apple slices.

"You're kidding," I said. "A year book?"

"No," she said. "Open it. It's a slam book."

"A what?"

I vaguely remembered slam books. Back in junior high, it was all the rage. One person would start a journal and then pass it to a friend and so on, until it was returned back to its owner. I opened the book and flipped through the pages. They were filled with short written passages—mostly from Michelle's school friends—each of whom had contributed something. There were little stories, bits of advice, doodles and drawings, poems and gossip, favorite songs, crushes on boys . . . all kinds of stuff.

"You're kidding. The artifact is nothing more than a slam book?"

Michelle nodded, grinning from ear to ear.

"That's it exactly. A slam book. Or Facebook, I guess. I don't know how else to describe it. It was amazing. One second I was standing next to you, the next I'm actually inside this thing. I was scared at first, but I must have fallen into a trance or something because I started seeing pictures. And get this, not only did I see them, but I could hear, and feel, and taste . . . and some other senses that I won't even try to describe. I couldn't if I wanted to. I don't think I could describe most of what I experienced. But it was like I was actually there, living these brief snippets of people's lives. I'll call them people although I tell you, Pete, most of them didn't look anything like us."

Michelle was crying now. "It was so beautiful. You can't even imagine. Even though it was only a few minutes for each person, I got to experience their lives. There was this weird octopus-like creature that lived deep in the ocean. It was so smart and really very funny. It was giant, but among its kind, it was tiny and an outcast. It found the sphere and got in just like I did. All these other people did as well. There was this cockroach-like monster on some really hot planet, and I could feel it. It was amazing. He sang his favorite song. There was also this fern-like plant thing—it was so loving! I've never felt that kind of love before. Each one of them had something to say. And there were so many . . . hundreds! I can't even begin to tell you all of them. But that's what it was. It's nothing more than a slam book. I'm not sure who started it, but one of them did. They sent it, and it's been visiting one planet after another, where it waits until it can find somebody who can leave a message, another entry in the slam book, and then it moves on."

I laughed. In a weird way, it made perfect sense. What better way to communicate between the vast distances than to send out a cosmic slam book? A galactic version of social media. Facebook between the stars.

"I can see why the government guys were not happy."

"No," she said, her eyes sparkling with amusement. "They weren't."

"So," I said. "What about you? What message did you leave for our cosmic brethren? Did you talk about us?"

Michelle flashed me a secretive smile. "Ah-ah, now *that's* private."

Preston Dennett became a voracious reader of speculative fiction at age thirteen, after discovering the books of Clifford Simak. Before he could drive, the walls of his bedroom became an A-Z library of sci-fi and fantasy. Since then, he has worked as a carpet cleaner, fast-food worker, data entry clerk, bookkeeper, landscaper, singer, actor, writer, radio host, television consultant, teacher, UFO researcher, ghost hunter, and more. In addition to writing about UFOs and the paranormal, he has sold dozens of speculative fiction stories to various venues such as Cast of Wonders: The Young Adult Speculative Fiction Podcast, *Daily Science Fiction*, *Pulphouse Fiction Magazine*, and more. In 2019, after submitting 46 times, he won second place in the Writers of the Future Contest, Volume 35. He currently resides in southern California where he spends his days finding new ways to pay the bills and his nights exploring the farthest edges of the universe.

https://prestondennett.weebly.com/

THRILLER,
HORROR & MYSTERY

BURY YOUR DEAD

Emily Astor

I opened my eyes, the clean scent of Alex's favorite t-shirt lingering in my nose.

"Come on!" Lana pulled me from my seat. "You're missing it!"

I stumbled after her and leaned against the railing, the white metal stingingly hot in the early morning sun, and watched the propellers noisily chop the blue-green water. As the ship launched from port, a wake of bubbles and waves unspooled behind us like one long ruffle stretching from land to stern.

"Thanks for taking me with you. It's not every day you win a cruise to paradise," I frowned and twisted the wedding ring around my finger. "I hope I don't ruin it for you."

"Not possible! Lemon," my best friend pivoted and put both hands on my shoulders, "it wasn't your fault, you know. Even if you had seen the driver, there was nothing you could have done."

"That was Alex's nickname for me." I looked up at the gray sky. "Lemon."

She sighed. "I know."

"And then the robbery a month later. They cleaned out our *entire* apartment—even the drain stopper from the kitchen sink! What kind of person steals a *drain stopper*?!"

"It's been a terrible year," Lana agreed quietly before suddenly brightening. "C'mon, let's stop this depressing talk and get margaritas!"

She pulled me across the upper deck grinning, so I smiled for her despite the rugged boulder resting in the expanding black crevasse of my being. I sat in a lounge chair near the bar and let the shrill screeches of delighted children splashing in the pool distract me into the present. I watched Lana order our drinks from an overly chipper bartender, his smile as plastic as the curvy cups in which he would hand us our margaritas.

I scanned the dozen or so oiled bodies lounging around the pool; it was curious that there weren't more passengers on deck. I wondered whether we were missing an attraction on another deck when something warm lightly tapped my arm. I glanced over, expecting to swat a bug. Instead, a little girl in a pink swimsuit looked at me expectantly, licking an ice cream cone covered with rainbow sprinkles, her index finger hovering in the air an inch from my pale skin. Drops of tan ice cream ran down her fingers, forming a sticky puddle next to my chair. Disgusted and annoyed, I waited for her to speak. Finally, she opened her mouth, but then shut it abruptly. After a moment, she licked her lips and tried again. "I like peanut butter ice cream."

"Yeah, I had a friend when I was your age that liked it, too." A crop of uninvited memories bobbed to the surface in my mind's eye: the cool spring breeze whisking through my friend's screened-in patio that made the daffodils in the garden dance; the sticky glaze of half-dried cream coating her face from the tip of her nose to the bottom of her chin; her grin and the tsking of her mother as she scrubbed her face clean with a damp washcloth. Sadness, heavy and dull, drummed a slow dirge in my gut. "A lot of people like peanut butter ice cream," I added flatly and turned away.

I could feel her eyes on me and hear her smacking ice cream and mushing it around in her mouth. Exasperated, I tossed back over and yanked the tassels on my cotton coverup. "Aren't your mom and dad around?"

"Not yet," she said, wiping her chin with the back of her hand. "They're still asleep."

"They let you run around by yourself?"

"I'm ten years old! Besides, they'll be here soon."

I felt a shove in my back and snapped around in my seat. An old man in a long black coat stood an arm's reach away. His gray-blue eyes were like spheres of wild flashing light from his gaunt face as he glared at me. His rust-brown skin was deeply creased, his hair a shock of white, and his hooked nose gave the appearance of a puffin's beak when he stood in profile.

"What's your problem?" I snapped.

Through clenched teeth, he mumbled something that could have been either an apology or a curse and limped away.

"That's the captain," she said as she crunched into the sugar cone, "Charon."

"Yeah, he seems like the kind of captain I'd get on vacation."

"Here!" Lana said breathlessly, pushing a margarita into my hands. "Sorry, the bartender was out of margarita mix and had to look for more; it took forever! What'd I miss?"

I turned to gesture at the girl, but she was gone. "Oh, nothing much," I shrugged, "except the captain knocked into me. An accident, I suppose."

"Rude!"

"He looks like an old-timey sailor like out of Moby Dick." I slurped my margarita, letting the sharp golden sensation of tequila snake down my throat.

"He must be the off-season captain." Lana spread her towel over the chair next to mine and smiled.

After five more margaritas, we made our way to the buffet. I picked up a tray and started browsing the salad bar, loading olives, peppers, and cheese on top of a few wilted pieces of romaine and arugula.

As I dispensed soda from the beverage kiosk, I noticed the ice cream girl sitting alone at a nearby table. She had a large chocolate cake in front of her. Holding her fork like a spear, she stabbed a piece of cake and shoved it into her mouth.

"Hi," she said, swallowing.

"What's your name?"

"Abby."

"Where are your *parents*, Abby?"

She shrugged and brushed a strand of hair out of her eyes, her finger leaving a streak of frosting across her cheek. "You'll have to choose soon, you know." She popped another piece of cake into her mouth and smiled up at me as she chewed.

·· ◆ ◆ ◆ ◆ ◆ ··

I jolted awake in our dark cabin and moaned. "I had the weirdest dream."

"You're up!"

"When did you become a morning person?"

"It's twelve-thirty in the afternoon," she said, opening a curtain. "And you missed the excursions yesterday."

"I thought the itinerary said the first two days were at sea?"

"They were."

"We boarded yesterday."

"Lemon, we boarded the day *before* yesterday. Sheesh, someone has had *a lot* to drink!"

"Are you sure?" I rubbed my face, trying to recount my movements over the last couple days.

"Yeah, you had like a zillion margaritas yesterday."

I cradled my head. "I don't know if I'm going to make it out."

"Oh no you don't," Lana said, whipping the sheet off my bed. "Get dressed. And I'm going to switch us to daiquiris because I don't know *what* those margaritas are doing to you!"

"Ok, ok!" I grumbled as I pulled on a red t-shirt and shorts.

"I vote we run a few laps on the track and then scope out the excursion options for the next port."

I followed Lana through the labyrinth of hallways to the stairs that led to the upper deck. A couple was eating lunch at the bar and a woman with a large floppy hat sat on the sun deck intently reading a well-worn paperback. We dumped our bottled water and towels on an empty table and approached the track.

"Is it me, or does it seem like there are even less people on this ship than when we boarded?"

"I bet a lot of people are at the buffet. People take that all-you-can-eat thing as a personal challenge."

The sun was hot on the upper deck, and I was beginning to think this run was a terrible idea. But before I could suggest smoothies by the pool instead, Lana took off. Half-heartedly, I forced myself to break into a light jog. After the first lap, I started thinking about all the runs Alex and I went on. With the cool ocean air on my skin, I closed my eyes, and I could almost feel him running beside me. The ship lurched suddenly and threw me into the railing. Before I could get my bearings, a table slid and slammed into my hip. An umbrella caught the wind and came at me, crashing into my chest before it flew overboard, and my body arched backwards.

Lana grabbed my wrist and pulled me towards her. "Are you ok?"

"Yeah," I gasped and took a breath. "Jeeze, I can't catch a break, can I?" I let out a dry laugh that felt like cold ashes in my throat.

Lana went for ice, and I rubbed the spot where the umbrella hit me, dreading the bruise. I reached for my water bottle and noticed a slip of paper sticking up from behind the label. I plucked it out and read the message scrawled in messy black ink: *Get off the ship*. I balled up the note and shoved it into my pocket. Goosebumps fired up my sitz bones to the crown of my head. I could feel the intense energy of Captain Charon's eyes on me, but when I surveyed the deck, he wasn't in sight.

•·•◆◆◆•·•

"You don't look good."

"I'll be fine. I just have to get back to my . . . ." I looked around at my surroundings, mystified. I was back in my bed.

Lana tucked a strand of hair behind my ear. "We came back to the cabin after you got clobbered with all that deck furniture."

"The last thing I remember is waiting for you to bring back ice and finding this note," I said, handing her the paper from my pocket. "I've missed hours! *Days!*" I rubbed my temples, desperately trying to pull any memory of yesterday out of the murky mire of my mind. "I must have been drugged. There's no other explanation."

Lana's face was stern, lips pursed as she read the note. "Something is going on," she agreed. "Why don't we go to the upper deck and talk this out."

"What is there to talk about?!" My voice was high and thin, and I hated the sound of it. I despised the fear that cloaked me but felt powerless to shake off the immense weight of it. "I'm being drugged—probably by that creepy-ass captain, God knows why!"

"You're right, Lemon. Why don't you get dressed while I find security, and I'll meet you by the pool with some lattes?"

I nodded and slipped on my sandals. Lana left as I riffled through my suitcase, realizing I had seriously underestimated how many clothes to bring. Once I found a clean tank top and skirt, I pulled them on and stepped into the hallway. I turned right as we always did to get to the upper decks but quickly lost my sense of direction after that. I cursed myself for not paying more attention when Lana led me around the ship. Bursts of frustration crackled through my body. I started knocking on cabin doors, but no one answered. A scream stuck in my throat but dissolved when I turned the corner and caught sight of the girl.

"Abby, thank God! Which way takes you to the upper deck?"

"There's only one way," she said in a sing-song voice.

"I'm not in the mood for games—"

"He's getting impatient."

"Who?!"

Abby mimed sealing her lips and tucked the imaginary key in her pocket.

"Tell me! Now!"

Her brown eyes solemn, she pointed to the door on her right. I opened it and ran up the steps two at a time. At the top, I flung the door open and nearly collided with Captain Charon. I pulled back, my nostrils tingling with the thick, charred scent of sea salt and fire.

"You stay away from me!"

He scowled. "I never should have let you aboard!" He bared his yellowed teeth and brandished a wooden oar from the folds of his coat.

"What are you talking about?" I backed away, noticing with sinking dismay that the deck was completely empty. "My friend won these tickets!"

The captain's steely eyes bored into mine. "No space on my ship is *won*." He raised his oar; I scampered away, keeping distance between us.

"Why are you trying to kill me?"

He looked at me for a moment, then threw his head back and howled with laughter. "I haven't laughed that hard since I made Columbus navigate the Styx," he wiped a tear from his eye. "See? I *do* have a sense of humor."

"Nah, he just thinks he does," Abby said in a bored tone, licking a red lollipop.

"Run, Abby!"

The captain lunged at me but missed. "Hades!" he cursed. "Will you stay still for *one second*?!"

"Pathetic," Abby said under her breath. "Ok, look," She put a hand on her hip and pointed at me with her lollipop. "What happened to the girl—the one I remind you of?"

"She died in a drowning accident when we were kids."

"What was her name?"

"I don't remember. I was only ten!"

"Think!"

It came slowly, "It was . . . Abby."

"Lemon," his voice pricked my ears.

I turned, and the oar hit me square in the mouth. I fell to the floor clutching my face.

"Yes!" Charon held his oar to the sky in triumph. "Got her!"

"Dammit! Was that necessary, Charon?"

He shrugged. "She wasn't making any progress on her own."

"You ok?" Alex asked, helping me to my feet.

"Oh my God!" I stared at him, forgetting about my throbbing mouth, and wrapped my arms around him. He smelled like bergamot and the moment before a thunderstorm when the atmosphere is charged and still. I felt his solid, warm body against my skin and cried.

Alex pulled back from me, keeping his arms around me. "How does your mouth feel?"

I held him tighter. "It's nothing a dentist can't fix."

"Are you bleeding or missing any teeth? Does it even hurt?"

I prodded each tooth carefully with my tongue; all of them were firmly in place. "Actually . . . no."

"Lemon, it's time. You have to choose to see what you refuse to."

"What are you talking about?"

"I'm talking about you chasing three tenants out of our old apartment," he said, nudging me playfully. "You kept moving everything around and scared them half to death!"

"Our apartment was burglarized . . ."

"No, Lemon," he said gently, "Both of us died in that collision."

"No, I didn't! Lana's with me, she'll tell you."

Alex paused. "Do you remember why I gave you your nickname?"

"Of course! The RA made us wear those stupid nametags around the dorm. My handwriting's so sloppy, you thought I wrote *Lemon*, but of course I wrote . . ."

He tucked a strand of hair behind my ear, and the ship came to an abrupt halt.

"She still owes me," Charon snarled.

I moved my tongue around my mouth and felt a slim circular piece of metal between my gums and cheek. I removed it, and a crudely pressed silver coin glinted back up at me from my palm. Charon snatched it and smiled as he tucked the coin away inside his coat.

Abby tugged my hand. "Race you to the deep end!" she stuck her tongue out at me and ran down the gangway.

Thick fog surrounded us. I squinted but couldn't make out anything beyond the ship. My eyes felt heavy and I trembled.

"Wait, I can't see what's out there!" I cried, gripping the railing, "I can't just *go* . . ."

"But we're already here, Lemon! Come on," Alex winked and held his hand out for mine, "everybody's waiting."

Emily Astor lives in Baltimore, Maryland and graduated Magna Cum Laude with a bachelor's degree in writing. She has 25 years of experience in business and creative writing and is releasing a series of novelettes on Amazon Kindle this winter. Emily's hobbies include painting, sports-inspired workouts, and hiking with her dog.

WORKAHOLIC

Ralynn Frost

My father was a workaholic. The old man had slaved his days away in the coal mines—proud to be doing his part to fuel Appalachia, but a stranger at the dinner table where my mother always kept a plate ready. They taught me as a child that hard, dedicated work was the path of righteousness, something to aspire to. Be devoted to your employers, and they'll be loyal to you. Earn your keep and they will reward you. In the end, all I earned was an empty pill bottle and this lousy pickaxe.

The blade was dull when I pulled it from the dark closet, stained with years of rust from neglect. A physical symbol of my labor's burden, the tool dragged after me, scraping against the rough tile floor of the office where I used to work. Admittedly, I was no longer sure whether the wake of red flakes left behind was corrosion or blood. Despite the bright, shining lights and the bitter silence, I could no longer distinguish between what was real and what wasn't. My former coworkers cowered under their desks while I shuffled. Quiet, as they had been when they all saw me drowning, and praying to the God that forsook us when I passed. One of the faceless screamed when the tip of the ax crashed through the wall of her cubicle. Removing it decapitated the kitschy kitten poster that bolstered everyone to "hang in there."

I did hang in there. I had gripped the edge of sanity with my fingernails.

Life hadn't always been about setting fixed interest reports on fire or terrorizing other employees at Wolfram & Deloitte. Once upon a time, I was a fresh-faced college grad with a chip on my shoulder and a point to prove. I was moving to succeed, make a name for myself in the big city, and do what my broken predecessor never could.

Naturally, I went to school and got myself a nice, over-priced degree to frame. I applied, and I interned. Above all, I did favors, groveled, and networked. I built an experienced resume for the sake of landing a job that would take me places. I wanted to produce money and friends, buy my fantasy penthouse high above the downtown skyline, and then drive back to my dusty rural town to show off the fruits of my efforts. I craved a big slice of that American dream.

I did what I was supposed to do. I did everything right. On the other hand, I wouldn't impress my dad with the severed head of my boss.

"911, help! Please help us! He's gone crazy, and he's going to kill us all!"

"That's funny hearing *you* ask for help, Nancy! What was it you told me? To suck it up, Buttercup?"

My laughter rang hollow, sounding choked, as if it were coming from someone else's throat. Similarly, it was someone else's blood-spattered hands swinging the blade. Splinters of shrapnel flew everywhere, the axe splitting the desk and Nancy too.

She had been the first employee I met at W&D. Nancy, the Assistant Manager, had shown me the break room, the coffee rules, and the way to my cubicle. The hours were long and grueling—undoubtedly like what I imagined my dad suffered when I would lie awake at night, listening for the sound of his beat-up truck to rumble home. Expectations were high and the pace swift, but I succeeded. With the intent of turning my workspace into a corner office, I completed all the assigned objectives with an accuracy and efficiency that garnered a smile from

Crusty Crowley, "Crusty" being a proper nickname for the Department Director when he wasn't around to hear. To show my value, the company rewarded me with a five-cent raise and another report to do since I was flourishing so well.

That was only the beginning. I worked faster and harder, multitasking my fingers across clacking keyboards. They applauded me for the excellence I provided. Again, the business repaid me with more tasks. Foolish and green, I offered my support to any who asked. Each accomplishment fell into a void that hungered for fulfillment.

"Yes, I will help you out of your jam. Yeah, I can take some of your load off. I know it's hard."

I came early, and I stayed late, skipping my lunch for the sake of productivity. That is to say, my life dwindled away, bathed in the ghastly blue light of computer monitors. Days warped into weeks, months, and then years. W&D passed me over for a promotion, the coveted leadership role hired out to personnel from outside the firm. Even so, it spurred me to work *more*, to keep my nose to the grindstone, hoping to gain satisfaction. By God, if my father could do it, so could I—until I collapsed in my gilded cage after closing time. With the lights off, the gentle hum of air conditioning was my only solace. Housekeeping found me with the L key lodged in my forehead, dial tone still bleating in my unconscious ear.

"Dehydration. Drink some water once in a while. I'm writing you a prescription for anti-anxiety medication and also a referral for nutrition counseling. You're underweight." The doctor that saw me mused over her laptop typing chart notes without even looking in my direction. She gave a hopeful outlook, but her only focus was on the digital screen separating us.

Drink. I programmed my smart watch to remind me to stay hydrated. Every two hours, it would flash the word at me. The consistent self-care resulted in a return to the normal frequency of bathroom trips. I developed a habit of holding conversations with myself during those times, perhaps as a way of keeping myself company.

"We need to remember to go to the Drug Aide later and get a refill."

"Who has the time?" I asked my visage in the lavatory mirror. While washing my hands, I noticed how the clothes hung from my bones, my eyes sunken and cheeks gone sallow. Likewise, the mimic's response was as despondent as I felt.

"This place is sucking the life out of you. Look at you. You're killing yourself over a nickel and the expectations that someone back home will pay attention."

"What do you know? I'm getting where *I* want to be. I just have to be patient and pay my dues like everyone else." And with that rally cry, I pulled a bottle with the RX symbol printed on the label from my pocket. Inside were a handful of little white bars, a career-saving medication that helped the world slow down. I smiled at myself in the reflection as I tossed one down the hatch and waved goodbye to all of my problems.

"Crowley wants to see you in his office."

Nancy's voice was grating as she popped her smarmy head over the wall of my cubicle. The only occasion she spoke to me was when something went wrong—typically so she could throw me under the bus or gloat over my faults. But when I looked up, Nancy no longer had a face. She was blank as a manikin in a department store, her skin stretched like plastic without eyeballs or a nose, only a gaping hole where her mouth should have been. Equal to the mindlessly gnashing jaws of a shark, the creature before me was created to consume. I forced myself to look away from the horror, squeezing my eyes shut to clear the hallucination. I swallowed hard and when I turned back again, the strange vision deteriorated. Her pudge snout returned to its rightful spot between her beady eyes.

"You're using the bathroom facilities excessively." Though we sat across from one another in his headquarters, Crusty didn't even glance my way, his pen fluttering signatures on document after document. "And I see here that you missed part of your shift this morning for a medical appointment. Try to schedule those things on your own personal time and don't waste any more of mine or the company's."

"Sir, I've been meaning to ask. Do you think maybe I could transfer some of my assignments to a different rep? There's really more on my plate than a person can reasonably handle."

"More work than you can handle? I see." Crusty put his pen down to lean in his chair and gazed at me with a dull expression. "I had high hopes for you when you first started out here. You seemed to fit in well and completed all of your tasks in a timely manner. We all thought you had a bright future. But now, you're lollygagging around in the restrooms, playing hooky, and trying to pawn your responsibilities off on others."

"I'm not trying to pawn . . ."

"The fact is, you are the *only* person in this department that doesn't seem to be able to handle their duties. No one else is complaining about there being too much work. No one else is having any problems with getting to their job and staying there. Maybe you need to take a good long look at yourself and determine if the real problem here isn't just you." Pop another pill.

I lost track of time. It was easy to do, surrounded by my three particle board walls with their colored sticky notes and the endless stack of folders on the corner of my desk. Nonetheless, the sun rose and then fell, rose and settled again while I stamped pages and entered data in an infinity of spreadsheet cells. I forgot what actual people looked like after being inundated by blank leach-like faces. Taking my second to last tablet, I peered into the hollow emptiness that remained in the medicine jar, knowing that I couldn't leave to pick up more. Deep within, I felt something crack.

"Hey Charlotte, do you think maybe you could take this tracking report back? It's been two years since you closed the Vinterberg file."

"That's not my thing." Another faceless devourer responded, not bothering to glance up from her phone where she was editing a selfie for her social media profile. She popped her head to the side and adjusted the color settings to magnify the shine of her teeth.

"But I got this from you."

"Yeah, and now it's yours. You just do such a better job with it than I do. I think it should stay yours. Besides, you love being helpful, right? It's a win-win for everybody." Pop another pill.

The pharmacist jumped as I banged on the window after closing hours. The lights were turned down to a dim glow, by which she had begun an inventory of shelved bottles.

"Hey! I need a refill!" I rapped on the glass, hoping to get a last-minute order before they went home for the evening. Although the white coat opened her transaction drawer in the drive-through to examine the prescription, she mumbled and shook her head as she stared into the blue glare of her computer monitor.

"This is a Schedule 4 drug. I can't refill this without a doctor's authorization, and I can't reach anyone at this hour."

"But . . ." I stammered for a moment, my memory painted with the darkness of the empty bottle. "I need this medication. I need this to go to work!"

"It's after midnight. I'm sorry, but there's nothing I can do. Call your doctor in the morning."

"I can't." My words fell on deaf ears as the drawer rescinded and my last hope fled to safer havens. The physician couldn't refill the meds without an office visit, and W&D wouldn't tolerate my leaving during drudging hours to fulfill such a personal obligation. I was on my own.

Sweat beaded on my brow line, my heart thumped in my chest, and a nauseous cramping sensation filled my gut as I sat at my desk later the next day. In addition, I blew on a steaming cup of coffee to aid the struggle against brain fog which overtook my functioning memory. The lights were too bright, the air too cold, and my skin was itchy.

"You look like hell."

"Thanks, Bob. I really needed you to tell me that."

"Somebody woke up on the wrong side of the bed today." A lump formed in my throat after looking up to watch my coworker walk away from my cubicle. Bob lost his face too, and so did everyone else in the department. They had all morphed into the expressionless demonic manikins, like a congregation of changelings.

"I told you this place was sucking the soul out of you." My reflection spoke from the bathroom mirror once I had finished vomiting in the back stall. "Look at yourself." My appearance was on the edge, the color having drained from my cheeks and left the remnants clammy. "They're feeding on you, all of them. They're *all* out to get you now. And once you're dead, they'll do it to the next sad sap that takes your spot."

"I have to do something. I need to stop this."

My facsimile lifted a shushing finger, eyes darting from side to side. No one bothered to glance in my direction as I sailed down the center aisle towards the door, their blank chattering faces focused on their monitors. I don't remember making it home, or returning for that matter, only sitting in the doorway of my closet staring at Dad's worn pickaxe. It was the last thing I had of him. His legacy molded to the shape of my hands. I felt it right that the old man should have a taste of vengeance too for all those years he wasted in the mines.

My father's weapon thumped behind me down the center aisle to the Big Man's suite. The view of the city skyscape from his corner perch was both awe-inspiring and, at the same moment, a dystopian ocean of steel and glass. Certainly the metropolis was an ocean floor teaming with life for the parasites to feed from.

"Mr. Crowley, I've been thinking." Suddenly, he wasn't as tall as I recalled his being when I came to work at W&D. The boss devourer knew I had come for him, standing at his desk to plead for his life as I entered the room with my axe poised in striking position.

"I don't think I fit in here at W&D after all. I would love to give you my resignation, personally."

Ralynn Frost is the Curator's Choice Award Winner for Horror. She knows how to send chills down your spine. Besides her murderous fictional work, Ralynn is a chemical engineer, an entrepreneur who develops web content, and a caffeine addict with a bloody edge.

HIM

Maria Rice

I wanted to scream but I couldn't. He had his fingers wrapped around my throat, clutching my vocal cords. The cold feeling of metal against my carotid. One wrong move and it would plunge deeply inside me, slicing the skin and severing the artery. I would bleed out. I knew I would.

had spent the last two months here. Or at least that's what I thought. It was easy to lose track of time. He used to feed me three times a day and I would know by the third meal that I had survived another day. But then the feedings became less and less frequent. Twice a day, then once a day. Now, I was lucky if I even got a sip of water. He would trick me and replace the water in the bottle with his own piss, forcing me to drink the whole thing while he watched me writhe in disgust. I knew it was urine the second he would hand it to me—the warmness of the plastic, the scent of expired rum. The first time I drank it, I remember choking on my own dignity and then spewing it all over the floor. He ripped out my hair, twisted it around his fingers, using it like a mop to clean up the floor. He said, "You made a mess, now it's time to clean it!" and then he laughed and laughed and laughed. He was laughing at my pain. Cackling at my pain. Tears streamed down my face. "I'm sorry, sweetheart," he said. "Let me make you feel better."

I knew what this meant. He always said it right before bedtime. Right before stripping me. Right before touching me. At first, it felt kind of good but now, I find myself numbing my body to the pain. It's the only way to survive.

He lived right above me. I never saw his house but I would hear him. I would hear glass shattering, gunshots, and groans as he satisfied himself. But the worst sound was the creak of the door opening and his steel toe boots hitting the old, wooden stairs. There would be a flash of light and how I prayed it would be the last light I saw before God would come down and save me. He never did, though. The only person who came down those stairs was him. He would come stumbling down the stairs, seemingly drunker with each step he took. The smell of rum was always on his breath, choking me. He tortured me with it. Each unopened bottle was stored in the basement. He would come down, grab one, gulp down the contents, and then shove the empty bottle inside me over and over again. Sometimes he would drop the bottle and the glass would shatter, but he didn't care. As long as it still had its neck, he'd shove it up me, chards facing in. I bled every night, but it was never enough to kill me. I prayed one day it would—one day that I would go to bed bleeding and never wake up. But my prayers were never answered. Each day my eyes opened and I cried knowing the tortures that awaited me.

And each day was worse than the last. But today, today was by far the worst. He came down with a knife. I didn't see it, but I felt it. He placed the cold metal over my heart and moved it down my body, through the folds of my naked skin. He wanted me to feel it. He wanted me to know it was there. He wanted me to know the power he had. And then, he stopped. For a split second, I didn't feel cold anywhere. But I knew it was still there. I knew he was still there. I could hear him breathing and I felt his sweat trickle from his beard and down onto my skin. Then, all of a sudden, I felt the knife go in me like an icicle. I froze for a second, and then I screamed, crying out in pain. He grabbed my neck, crushing my trachea. Then he took the knife out from inside me and shoved it in my mouth. It tasted like blood. *Back and forth, back and forth, back and forth.* He laughed when he felt me swallow, his fingers still clenched around my neck. Then he ripped the knife out of my mouth, swiftly slicing my cheek. Blood spurted everywhere. I felt the cold metal against my carotid. One wrong move and it would plunge deep inside me, slicing the skin and severing the artery. I would bleed out. I knew I would. This was it. I needed to end my misery. I needed to cut myself on that knife. It was hard to move, he was grasping me so tightly. If I could just get the right angle. I pressed harder and harder against the metal, feeling it break the first folds of my skin. I was almost there, just a few more inches to go . . .

·•✦◆✦•·

I woke up in the hospital. When I first opened my eyes, I thought I was in heaven. I heard a distant voice, "Gracie, honey."

I recognized that voice.

"Mom!" I cried.

"Yes Gracie, it's me. We're going to get you out of here."

"We?" I questioned.

"My boyfriend, Gracie. Don't you remember him?"

Just then, the smell of rum filled the air and I heard that dreaded sound again. The sound of steel toe boots. "Hi, sweetheart." I froze. It was him. It was *Him.*

He was even uglier than I pictured. His eyes were crooked and covered in soot. His lips were pale and dry. His beard was thick with an orange tint. He was shorter than his shadow had appeared to be in that basement, but his fingers were much fatter. "What's wrong, honey?" my mom asked.

I gulped. "I—I'm sorry, I must've zoned out for a second."

"It's okay. Do you remember anything?"

Yeah. I thought. I remember exactly who did this to me. I remember exactly what he did.

But I was too weak to admit it, intimidated by his smug gaze. "No, I don't remember anything," I lied.

"Someone was hurting you."

"A man?" I asked.

"Yes," my mom said. "An older man. He had a knife. Do you remember that?"

Of course I remembered. How could I ever forget?

"I remember being hurt with a knife."

"No, honey. The police said you weren't hurt with the knife. He was holding it over you when the police shot him, but they misfired and the bullet went through your cheek."

No. I thought. This isn't from a gun, it was from a knife, his knife.

"The man got away, but the police want to ask you a few questions about him, okay?"

Okay?! This whole thing wasn't okay.

"We'll be here the whole time," she said reassuringly.

I was about to speak up when the police walked in. "Hi, I'm Detective Gomez. I'm going to ask you a few questions if that's okay?" I nodded. "I know this is going to be hard, but I really need you to tell the truth."

The truth! How was I supposed to tell the truth with him standing right next to me? He was practically breathing down my neck and it brought me back to that mattress. The dingy scent. The dust. The blood. The semen. It was stained. No, I was stained.

"Grace? Do you have something you want to say?" the cop questioned.

I pointed my finger towards him, but no words came out.

"Him?" the police officer asked.

"Oh, sweetie. Do you want me to hold your hand?"

I wanted to barf at his words. And his looks. He was staring at me. Straight in the face. And then he moved his gaze down. Something flashed out of the corner of my eye. I turned my head and then I saw it. The knife. He had the knife fastened in his waistband and he was holding his jacket back just enough so I could see it. He wanted me to know it was there. He wanted me to know the power he had. He wanted me to know what would happen if I said anything.

"No one hurt me."

"So, he never hurt you?"

"He did." I said as he tugged at his waistband. "I mean . . . he didn't."

"I know this is hard, Grace. You can trust me."

I'll never trust anyone again! He made sure of that!

"Do you remember what he looked like?"

"He was old a . . . and a little larger I think." I was fumbling for words as tears began to stream down my face. "I really don't know who, I'm sorry."

"Can't you see you're hurting her?!" my mom cried.

"I'm just doing my job, ma'am."

"Well, you're done! She needs to rest."

"One hour. She can have one hour to rest and then I really need her to answer some more questions."

"Thank you!" my mom said as she led the officer out of the room.

"Go get yourself some food, Kathleen. I'll stay here with Gracie." He said this with a dirty smile on his face.

"It's okay, I want to make sure she's safe."

"I'll keep her safe." I looked at him, then at my mom.

"Is that okay with you honey?" she asked.

No, it's not! Please, don't leave me.

I looked back at him and saw the knife again. I gulped. "Yeah, it's . . . it's fine."

My mom bent over and gently kissed my forehead. I wanted to grab her head and whisper everything to her. I had so much to say, but I just couldn't figure out how to say it. Not with *him* standing in the corner. "I'll be back Gracie. I love you, forever and always." That was our thing. Forever and always. But today, it didn't feel like that. She was abandoning me and she had no idea.

As soon as she walked out of the room, I regretted not saying anything. There was nothing I could do now. I closed my eyes and prayed. Prayed that my mom would come back soon. Prayed that nothing would happen while she was gone. Prayed that he would leave me alone. But then, I heard the clunk of his steel toe boots hitting the floor. His footsteps were getting louder and louder. He was coming closer and closer. I kept my eyes shut tightly, but I could feel him coming closer. I could taste the rum as he exhaled over me. He lifted one leg and then the other, inviting himself into the bed with me. I couldn't do anything to stop him. He unbuckled his rusty belt. I could hear the buckle tap against the side of the bed. Then, I heard a zip. His laughter was coming next. I knew it would. This is how it always went. But this time was different. This time, this time I heard a groan. A groan and then silence. I squinted as I opened my eyes and there it was. The knife. Lodged in his chest. I screamed and then I cried. Tears of joy or tears of sadness? I wasn't sure. He was dead. I should be happy. But a part of me wished he would've suffered longer. That he would've endured my pain. That he would've felt what I felt. That he . . .

"Grace! What have you done?" My mom screamed, as she ran into the room.

"I . . . I didn't Mom." But her eyes weren't listening. She was fixated on something else. I looked down to match her gaze. I gasped. My hand was covered in blood. And I . . . I was holding the knife.

Maria Rice is a recent graduate from the College of Saint Rose, receiving a dual bachelor's and master's degree in adolescence education: social studies and special education. She has chosen to jumpstart her teaching career at a local charter school, although she plans to continue writing in her free time. Maria also enjoys hiking, traveling, and spending time with her dog, Bailey.